# J.D. NETTO

# HENDERBELL

## THE SHADOW OF SAINT NICHOLAS

# HENDERBELL

## THE SHADOW OF SAINT NICHOLAS

Henderbell: The Shadow of Saint Nicholas
© Copyright 2019 by J.D. Netto

Cover design © 2019 by J.D. Netto Designs
Book design and production by J.D. Netto Designs
Tree vector: Shutterstock

*To my sister, who taught me to be strong.*

# ENZO

# CHAPTER 1

I always found comfort while staring at the Christmas tree in our living room during the holiday season.

After a miserable day listening to teachers blabber about subjects I didn't care for, I got home, tossed my backpack on the floor, sunk in the couch, and hit play on my favorite playlist, ready to split my attention between social media and the Christmas lights.

Seeing the lit pine tree reminded me of the days when my parents actually enjoyed each other's company, and my house was somewhat peaceful. My family used to come together on Christmas eve, alternating every year between our place and my grandparents' house in Dorthcester, Massachusetts.

But everything changed after some big fight four years ago. Now all I had left were the usual phone calls from my

2 | J.D. NETTO

grandparents saying they weren't going to make it or my parents' predictable excuses.

There was always talk of sending my sister and I to Dorthcester for Christmas, but I knew better than to get my hopes up.

The last four years in my house consisted of watching my parents fight and bicker. Part of me blamed the alcohol, which became my dad's top priority after the event. The other blamed my mom for being so passive about the whole situation. Then I blamed myself for actually despising their company—even when they weren't going at it, which was a rare thing to see.

During this time of the year, if I weren't hanging out by the tree, I was locked in my room, drawing, writing, and reading. I enjoyed escaping my world. And yes, the intense all-year-round heat in Palmsand, Florida, didn't inspire me to go out much. I wasn't a beach person since tanning for me meant turning as red as a bell pepper.

High school didn't help either. During classes, my mind would wander, along with my pen. I became a professional at drowning everyone out so I could sketch a dragon, a castle, a mountain, or some form of magical creature on any piece of paper in front of me.

But my love for art and my apparent inability to grow out of it led me to loneliness.

While scrolling down my social media feed, I found a throwback photo of Billy holding his sketch of a medieval knight. He actually won an award for that drawing on seventh grade. But the thing that intrigued me the most was the fact he cut me off the picture, leaving himself and Cliff on full display.

The caption: *Friends until the end.*

My friends abandoned me on freshman year. Their reason: Enzo stayed weird. I *stayed* weird. These were the same people who would come over so we could go on bookstore trips. These were the guys who introduced me to movie scores and writing playlists on the internet.

I scrolled down to read the comments on the photo.

CliffUpYours: *You cut out Fairy Enzo. You savage.*

BillyVanilly20: *Enzo who?*

I hit the block button and laid my phone face-down on my chest, turning up the volume of the music.

The mockery around the things I liked was the perfect recipe to drain my creativity or desire to do anything. You're told to ignore the comments, and even though you do, they're like drips on a rock; the damage imminent.

My attention returned to the tree, the peaceful sight disturbed by a shadow outside the window. My heart raced as I sat up on the couch and hit pause on my music, my headphones resting on my neck. I knew he was drunk because he walked like a wobbling sausage. I didn't hear his car park on the driveway, which meant someone dropped him off.

The wooden steps of the stairs leading to the porch creaked as my mom rushed down. Her presence brought along a strong stench of cigarettes. Her hair was tied into a bun, wisps falling by her ears. Her eyes red, chin quivering.

"You're not getting in here!" she shouted, grasping the door handle. "Enzo, go to your room! Make sure your sister stays in hers."

I jumped from the couch at the sound of my dad thudding against the door.

"You're sleeping on the street today!" Mom screamed.

Keys rattled on the other side.

"Let me in, Evelyn," Dad drawled, unlocking the door.

"You've been gone since last night! It's almost dinner time!" My mom held one foot out, her knee pressed against the door. "You're staying out there tonight." She looked at me, eyes fuming. "Enzo, I told you to go to your room!"

I couldn't just leave her. I feared Dad was going to do what he always does whenever he was drunk.

"Evelyn, quit whining and let me in," he insisted, pushing the door with a shoulder.

"What's going on?" Ava appeared on the stairs, her faithful companion, a brown teddy bear named Mr. Wombington, in her grasp. She wore her favorite pajamas covered in pink and white stripes. Her brown hair was tied back, wisps falling over her eyes.

"Ava, sweetheart, go—"

He slammed the door, thrusting Mom back.

Ava screamed.

"What do you think you're doing?" I marched toward him, body trembling with anger. "You can't just spend the night out and come back home like everything is okay."

"I pay your bills, kid." He stabbed a finger at my eye level. "And this is my house. You better shut up or I'll kick you out." He fell on the couch. I cringed at the smell of alcohol.

"Enzo." Mom got on her feet, eyes glistening. "Please go upstairs with your sister."

"Are you going to be—"

"Now, Enzo!" She shouted.

I ran up the steps, grabbed Ava's hand, and dragged her to my room.

"Bane, I can't fuc— "

I shut the door behind me before Ava heard another cuss word.

"Are you alright?" I asked behind ragged breaths.

"You don't have to look at me like that." She sat on my bed, fixing her hair behind her ears. "I've heard the F-word a million times already. I'm nine, not stupid. "

"What if we listen to some music?" My voice trembled as I approached my vinyl collection. I flipped through them with fumbling hands.

"Mr. Wombington and I would like that," she said.

I found an Elvis Presley Christmas vinyl and played it at a decent volume. I sat at the foot of the bed as my parents' screams turned to distant muffles.

"I can always hear them, you know." She kept her head down, her thumb caressing the teddy bear.

"I know." My heart tried to pry my chest open.

"Then why play the music?" she asked. "We know they're fighting."

"So we can pretend everything is okay," I replied to the sound of *White Christmas*.

When I was a kid, I pretended I was off in some far away land, fighting dragons, riding horses, and meeting all sorts of magical creatures. I'd spend hours in my room drawing the strangest beings, all very real in my head. Pretending used to be a joyous escape. But as I grew older, pretending became a sorrowful excuse to avoid real life. And this was mine.

Maybe pretending was the thing that hurt me the most. I wouldn't have to face my reality as long as I could keep on pretending. I glanced at my bookshelf on the opposite side of the room and shuddered.

I lowered the volume of the record player when I noticed Ava asleep on my bed, holding her teddy bear as if it could keep her alive.

I got on my feet and pressed my ear on the door, trying to hear any screaming or yelling. It was quiet.

I opened the door and tip toed my way downstairs.

The Christmas ornaments were shards scattered in the living room. The tree was on top of the couch, its star still clinging to the pine's tip. The sight became a blur as tears welled in my eyes. I thought about my sister and what she would think. I thought about how unfair all of this was. I feared the part of me that wished them away.

"Mom? Dad?" I yelled, dodging the shards. Blood boiled in my veins as I walked out the door.

I stepped out into the porch, the Florida humidity greeting me—Mom's car still on the driveway.

"You can't keep doing this to those kids." Someone said in the distance. I followed the voice, spotting my neighbor, Ms. Lumber, sitting on her porch with my parents. "If you keep this up…"

I hurried back to the house before hearing the rest. With one last look around the living room, I retreated to my bedroom.

I sat on the floor and reclined my back on the foot of my bed. It was time to stop pretending. I crawled toward my bookshelf and grabbed my sketchpad hidden between a few books.

"Time to say goodbye," I whispered.

Anger erupted as I marched down the stairs, walked into the kitchen, and ripped the notebook apart, tossing it in the trash.

# CHAPTER 2

"You guys have everything?" Mom asked, a cigarette in hand.

"You're smoking this early in the morning?" I scowled while scrolling through a couple of digital drawings on the discovery page of my feed.

"Are *you* going to start acting up this early in the morning?" Wrinkles appeared on her forehead.

"At least I'm not inhaling cancer." I shuffled on the couch.

She gave me a nod of disapproval, heading to the stairs, spreading the stench of her cigarette even more. The smell always made my stomach churn.

"Did you have to throw out the tree?" She halted at my words. "Maybe we could've fixed it together."

"Why?" She glanced over her shoulder. "You and your sister will be gone. You're the ones who care about that stuff."

"Gotcha," I mumbled as she disappeared up the stairs. It was as if our absence was a relief to her.

Our bags were beside me. After last week's episode, they decided to ship my sister and me to Dorthcester to spend Christmas with our grandparents. I was honestly surprised they were coming through this time. When I questioned the reason, she said she and my father had a few personal things to do during Christmas week. She probably thought I didn't see the divorce papers on the counter the day before yesterday.

When younger, I used to think divorce would never knock on my parents' doors until their marriage cracked in front of my eyes. And as the years went on, life kept showing me how unpredictable it could be.

Ava and Mom appeared on the stairs.

"I'm actually excited to see Grandma." Ava held her teddy bear in one arm and her heavy pink jacket on another. She wore blue leggings and a beige knitted sweater. "I'll get to show Mr. Wombington their house!"

"Do you even remember what it looks like?" I tucked my hands inside the pockets of my favorite black sweatshirt. "It's been, what, four years since we've been there?"

"I was five, Enzo, not dumb." She scowled.

"Leave her alone, please." Mom opened the door to the porch, car keys in hand. "I don't have the patience to deal with nonsense today. Now come on."

"Where's Dad?" Ava asked.

"Probably drinking his life away somewhere," Mom replied. "Enzo, you packed your drawing kit?"

Rage gripped me like a snake. "Like you didn't see it in the trash last week."

"I really didn't—mind grabbing the bags?" She reclined on the doorway with a frown.

"Whatever." My eyes rolled to the back of my head.

"It was about time you gave up these childish things. You'll be going to college in a couple of years. Time to think about the future. Spend time on things that actually matter."

I covered my ears with my noise-cancelling headphones, put on my backpack, grabbed the bags, and reeled them past her.

"You'll thank me in a couple of years." Her voice was a muffle.

Mom made no effort to talk during the drive. Ava watched some cartoon on her tablet while I listened to a shuffle mix. To my delight, I forgot to charge my headphones. My music died the moment we parked by the terminal doors.

"Enzo, keep an eye on Ava," Mom said as I unbuckled my seat belt.

"Will do." I was out of the car before I finished speaking.

"Bye, Mom," Ava said, standing beside me with Mr. Wombington.

Mom waved and said, "Close the door."

"Think she'll be okay?" Ava asked, watching the car drive away.

"To be honest, I'm just relieved we're going to be away from them for a while."

"That's not a nice thing to say," she mentioned.

"They haven't been the nicest of parents, have they?"

A shrug was her response.

A weight was lifted from my shoulders once the car was no longer in view. I wouldn't have to witness the arguments, the fights, and the smell of alcohol for the next few days. Though I had always pictured us returning to Dorthcester as a family, I was willing to accept whatever life had given at the moment.

# CHAPTER 3

"What are you most excited about?" Ava asked the moment I grabbed our bags from the carrousel. In her hand was the pink astronaut jacket she had brought on the plane.

"Right now?" I frowned. "I'm excited to get out of this crowded airport."

"I mean, what are you most excited about for this trip?" She puckered her lips.

"The certainty our parents won't be going at it on Christmas." I smirked.

She clearly expected a different answer. Her gaze turned to a group of people reeling their bags in front of us. She squeezed her teddy bear and took in a deep breath.

"Hey, sorry." She looked at me. "I'm excited we'll get to spend some time together—away from the screaming and the yelling. That's what I meant to say."

"Me too," she whispered, putting on her jacket.

I despised carrying anything on the plane besides my backpack. And even if I was aware of the fact my sweatshirt wasn't enough to shield me from the cold, I decided to brave the frigid temperature.

"I hope they're here already," I muttered.

The freezing Massachusetts air greeted me and my sweatshirt. I didn't remember it ever being this cold.

"Holy…" My breath was smoke. There was no way I could've missed them. My cheeks burned at the sight of them outside of their car, holding a bright green sign that read, '*We live to embarrass our grandkids.*'

Ava ran toward them with arms spread out.

I cringed, keeping my head down. A battle raged in me. I was happy to see them again after four years, but they had also been but a memory since.

"Grandma!" She threw her arms around her.

"Ava, you're so big!" Grandma squealed.

"Enzo." Grandpa gave me a hug. "It's been too long."

"Hey, Gramps," I patted him on the back. His salt and pepper hair was combed back, beard perfectly trimmed. He wore a red button-down under his black coat, and dark jeans that matched the black frame of his glasses.

"You look good, Enzo." He smiled. "You're almost as tall as I am."

"Well, it has been a while." I scowled. "But you look good too. And don't take this the wrong way, but do you guys ever age? Happy to see we have good genes, but..."

"You're too kind, sweetheart." Grandma's eyes glistened. Her outfits usually made her the center of attention wherever she was. Today was no different. To celebrate our arrival, she had on a bright yellow blouse, orange lipstick, silver pants, blue boots, and a white faux fur coat.

"My turn." Ava pushed me aside and hugged Grandpa.

"Look at you." Grandma cupped my face with her hands. "So handsome."

"Thanks." I forced a smiled. "I like the glasses."

"Oh, these?" The pink frame emphasized her hazel eyes. "They didn't have anything brighter so I had to settle."

Grandpa tossed our bags in the trunk of the car and said, "Alright, we're ready to go. We have to hurry since we aren't allowed to park here."

"We're supposed to get a pretty big storm tonight," Grandma said as we drove away to the sound of some random radio news program. "Glad your flight arrived before the madness."

"So Enzo," Grandpa started, his brown eyes reflected on the rear-view mirror. "Still drawing and writing?"

"Not really," I replied. Ava turned her head toward me, eyes wide. "Time to focus on other things."

"You gave up art forever?" Ava asked, disappointed. "I thought you threw away your notebook because you were angry, not because you were giving up."

"Time to grow up, sis," I said, my mom's words echoing in my head.

Grandpa took a sip from his massive coffee cup with great determination.

"Where's this coming from?" Grandma nodded in disapproval. "You're sixteen. You have plenty of time to explore all of your avenues before making a decision like that."

"Exactly," I said. "I'm sixteen. And there comes a time when one has to stop pretending. I better start early."

"How are your friends doing?" Grandpa tapped on the steering wheel.

"They're probably doing something with the other popular kids." I scratched the side of my head. "At the moment, Enzo here is a loner."

"Whatever happens, don't change yourself to please other people." Grandpa scowled, probably noticing my vacant stare. "Change yourself for you."

Heat flushed through my body. "Are you guys going to start lecturing me this early on the trip?" I let out a long breath. "At least save something for the next couple of days."

"No, of course not." Grandma laced fingers with Grandpa as the car slowed down due to a traffic jam.

"Looks like we're going to be stuck here a while. How about some Christmas music?" Grandpa changed stations until finding one playing Sinatra's rendition of *I'll Be Home for Christmas.*

"Love this song," Ava squeezed her teddy bear.

"This one is for you, Enzo!" Grandpa swayed his head to the melody.

My urge was to tell him of the memories this song sparked in me. Listening to it was like watching a live video of the day he dressed up as Santa and gave me my first sketchbook. But I chose silence. Sharing those memories would be the same as watering a dead seed.

A wide collection of Christmas classics played on the radio as the four of us remained quiet. Grandpa kept glancing at the mirror, my eyes averting his gaze every time. A mixture of happiness and anger took me. I was happy to be here where many of my happy memories were made, but angry as to how they acted as if it hadn't been four years since we last saw each other.

After leaving Boston, trees and hills replaced the concrete buildings and cars. An orange and purple sunset painted the horizon. Social media was flooded by photos of people from school going away on vacation with their families.

A text notification from my father appeared on the screen.

*Dad: Did you arrive okay?*

*Me: All good here.*

*Dad: Your sister?*

*Me: Beside me.*

*Dad: Have a good time. Tell them I said hello.*

*Me: Will do.*

This is what I wanted to write instead: *No, Dad, I'll tell them of how drunk you were last week. I'll also tell them of how you spent an entire day wandering around town and then you came home and threw Mom on the floor, reeking of alcohol.*

Ava's eyes were glued to her tablet. She still watched the same cartoon series from the plane.

I put the phone in my pocket. The landscape outside was now a familiar sight. There was an abandoned church that always captured my attention. It was surrounded by trees, its walls covered in cracks, its ceiling gray, full of holes. When younger, I imagined creatures crawling out of its eerie structure, infiltrating the town, searching for kids to devour.

"Welcome, welcome," Grandma said, the sign *Welcome to Dorthcester* in view, its right side partially hidden behind a maple tree.

Quaint houses emerged, encircled by pine and oak. Christmas lights, Santa inflatables, and Rudolphs were everywhere. The town looked like something out of a Hallmark movie.

"I absolutely love the Santa inflatables this year." Grandma pointed at one dressed in beach clothes. "I think they accurately depict him. Especially the gut."

"I think these Santas are awfully lonely. Maybe we need to have Mrs. Claus inflatables made as well," Grandpa said. "Maybe she could wear something that doesn't make her look like a bag of M&Ms?"

"At least she'd look delicious." Grandma puckered her lips.

"Good one. But why call the guy Santa? He has the most amazing name on the planet," he continued.

"Are you saying that because your name is Nicholas?" Ava asked, Mr. Wombington in her arms.

"Of course. I'd much rather be called Saint Nicholas than Santa."

"What a strange conversation." I facepalmed as they shared a laugh.

"I wish Santa was real." Ava squeezed Mr. Wombington

"I wish many things were real." I observed the crowds as we drove by the local market. The parking lot was overrun by people with shopping carts stacked with brown plastic bags along with cases of water and bags of salt.

"See how they get us to spend our money every time there's a storm?" Grandpa wagged his head. "They exaggerate on their predictions so we can buy things we don't need."

"At least we'll have a white Christmas tomorrow," Grandma said.

"Mr. Wombington, wait until you see the house!" Ava held the teddy bear close to her cheeks, her tablet beside her. "It's so beautiful in there."

A rush of adrenaline jolted through my body as we drove up the hill, the yellow house now in view, surrounded by towering trees. The first thing I spotted was the pine wrapped in Christmas lights with a neon sign that read *A Very Griffin Christmas*. The words were shaped like an arch, the first and last letters larger than the rest. Under the pine tree were four deer sculptures illuminated by two light strobes.

From the gable hung falling icicles glimmering in white and gold. The columns and railings of the porch were wrapped in golden tinsels and lights that shifted from gold to red and then silver.

I fought away a brief smile, my heart tightening as the ghosts of my past appeared around the house. I could see my dad and I playing in the snow, my mom telling us to go inside so we wouldn't catch a cold, Ava making snow angels.

My thoughts were disturbed by my phone vibrating. Billy sent me a photo via direct. It was him holding a bottle of beer, sunglasses on his face. On the picture, he wrote: *Am I your dad yet?*

The picture was like a punch in my stomach. The phone became a blur as tears welled in my eyes. I took in a deep breath as we parked on the driveway.

"Be careful, Ava. There might be black ice," Grandma shouted as soon as Ava hopped out of the car. Mr. Wombington's long legs dragged on the brick pathway as she ran toward the house, jumping up the steps leading to the front door.

Grandpa popped the trunk as Grandma followed Ava.

I put the hood of my sweatshirt over my head, and stepped out, backpack in hand. I shuddered as a cold breeze greeted my cheeks. The trees around me swayed to the wind, spreading the smell of pine in the air.

"I could really use your help here," Grandpa said, holding up the door of the trunk.

"Sorry, got distracted." I rushed to his side.

"You alright, buddy?" He grabbed one of the bags.

"I'm okay." I grasped the other, my breath steam.

"Are you sure?" He lifted the handle of the bag.

"Yes, Grandpa," I replied with a scoff. "Thought I had spotted a squirrel or something. But I'm alright."

"Are you sure you didn't perhaps see a gnome running through the woods?" He continued as we wheeled the bags to the house. "Or maybe there was a dragon somewhere? How about—"

"I appreciate the effort." I halted, brows pulled together. "But you can't just talk to me like I'm still a child. You've been gone a long time. Aside from a few calls and random texts, you've been pretty much a memory for the past four years."

He stared as if gazing at a corpse. The corner of his lips dropped down, his mouth now pressed into a line. I waited for him to say something, but he remained quiet, rooted to his spot.

With a nod of disappointment, I continued on toward the house.

# CHAPTER 4

The world seemed to slow down once I entered the living room, Grandpa behind me. The Christmas tree was by the fireplace—the same spot from four years ago, decorated in tones of red and gold. Wooden ornaments shaped like an elk's head clung to the branches wrapped in golden lights, surrounded by birds, stars, and snowflakes.

"I love this smell," Ava sniffed the air. "It smells like cinnamon pie."

"Your grandma insists on buying candles that smell like food." Grandpa rested an elbow on the handle of the bag, his eyes averting mine.

"Don't listen to him," Grandma sat beside Ava.

Another direct message, but this time, it was from Craig. Seeing his name on my phone screen was like poking a hole on my chest.

"Everything alright there?" Grandma asked, probably noticing my frown.

"Yeah." I held the power button until the phone shut off. "Everything is okay."

My eyes shifted to the tree in an attempt to sway my mind away from the message. I observed each ornament, two of them catching my attention more than the others. They were placed at the center of the pine, both shaped like an H with antlers. One was gold and the other silver.

I approached the objects, my reflection displayed on their surface. "Are they made of glass?"

"Crystal, actually," Grandpa replied. "Those are very special. They were given to the family by someone very important."

"Really?" I held the silver one between my fingers, the reflection of my dark eyes staring back at me.

"Yes." He grabbed both bags. "Now if you all don't mind, I'm going to bring these bags upstairs."

"I can give you a hand, Gramps," I said, releasing the ornament.

"I got it," he replied behind a grunt, walking up the stairs.

"Neither your mother and father wanted them," Grandma continued. "So we kept them."

"They're so pretty," said Ava.

"I think—" A dry cough interrupted Grandma's words, her face as red as a shrimp.

"Are you okay, Grandma?" I asked as she struggled to catch her breath.

"I'm alright." Her voice scraped her throat. "It's just a cold." She turned to Ava. "Feel like making cookies?"

"Yes, yes, yes!" Ava darted to the kitchen, leaving Mr. Wombington on the floor of the living room.

"Coming, Enzo?" Grandma asked, fixing her pink glasses over her nose.

"In a few," I replied.

The living room suddenly felt like a haunted house. I'm not sure if they kept the tree in the same spot hoping to spark good memories from the past, but the sight was a reminder of the home I once had. I wanted to talk about the divorce letters. I wanted to ask them if they ever tried to make peace with my parents after the fight. I wanted to ask them why they kept their distance. I feared all the answers would trigger a disagreement between us. The last thing Ava needed was to see another fight break out on Christmas.

I took in a sharp breath at the sound of Grandpa's steps creaking down the stairs.

"Bags are in your rooms." He walked to the fireplace and grabbed a box of matches sitting on the mantel.

"Cool."

"How's your sister doing with all this divorce talk?" He knelt in front of the hearth and lit a pile of crumbled newspaper and wood in the firebox.

"Ah, so you know," I said.

"Well, since you didn't want me to treat you like a kid, I thought we could talk about present struggles." He threw a few more pieces of wood in the fire.

"And you had to pick this subject," I added.

"Your father called this week," he continued, sitting on the couch, beckoning me closer with a wave. "And I'm not going to pretend like your grandma and I weren't expecting the news."

"Ava's okay." I sat beside him. "Sometimes I think she doesn't get it, but other times I think she pretends she doesn't," I said. "We all have to see the world for what it is at some point in our lives, right?"

"And what is the world to you, Enzo?" There it was, the stare that could pierce my soul like a blade, and it still had the same effect, even if absent for the past few years.

"I can't cuss in front of you." I shrugged.

"Let me share something I've learned. You may take this however you'd like. The world we see in our minds become our reality. Yes, we have to fight against darkness every once in a while, but those who persevere get their reward."

"What kind of reward did you get by persevering on staying away?"

He pressed his lips into a line, face rigid. "I won't try to apologize or explain. There are things you don't know—things you *shouldn't* know yet." My posture stiffened once he laid a hand on my shoulder. "I was going to wait a while to bring this up, but this house is open in case you and your sister want to stay here. I know I have no right to offer such a thing, but I thought I'd lay the option on the table."

"Are you serious?" My heart beast faster. "But what about Mom and Dad?"

"I'll talk to them." He frowned. "The divorce is their business, and neither you nor Ava need to be caught up in it."

Though thankful for his offer, and no matter how much I wanted to escape my life in Palmsand, I couldn't ignore the fact they weren't the same people from four years ago—at least not to me. "Can I think it over the weekend?"

"Of course." He retrieved his hand away from my shoulder and folded his arms. "But enough with the heavy talk. It's Christmas Eve and you and your sister are finally spending the holidays with us." He scrunched his face and smirked as if hiding a secret.

"What?" I asked with a grin.

"Surprised you haven't noticed it. Look up the fireplace."

Above it was something I didn't expect to see—the drawing I gave him for Christmas years ago. When I was six, I used up all of my crayons to draw that picture of Santa riding a dragon. The drawing was inside an ornamental golden frame.

"It's pretty clear I couldn't color within the lines back then."

A cold breath brushed the nape of my neck. I looked over my shoulder. My body tensed at the sight of a pair of dull gray eyes on a human-shaped shadow standing at the foot of the stairs.

"*I found them*," said a croaky voice in the air. "*The grandchildren are here.*"

Darkness crawled around me, hiding everything but the framed drawing on the wall and the eerie eyes.

"*I know you can hear me, prince,*" the voice continued as the pair of eyes disappeared.

Words became a whistled melody, followed by the chiming of bells. Screams, grunts, and the sound of clanging metal invaded my ears. They were joined by the neighing of horses and a bestial roar. The darkness was sucked up into the air as a voice whispered, *"You are cursed."*

# CHAPTER 5

The frame still hung above the fireplace. There was no one on the stairs. My heart pounded so fast, I thought it was going to burst out of my body.

"Enzo." Grandpa was still on the couch, a puzzled look on his face. "Are you alright? You've been standing there, staring into nothing."

"Oh, yeah." I cleared my throat, my attention shifting between his face and the stairs, my pulse beating in my ears. "Sorry, my mind wandered off. I just…didn't know you kept the drawing."

"You look pale." He stood to his feet. "Are you sure you're okay?"

"I just think I'm tired from the trip." I chuckled, my hands curling into fists. "Nothing a good night's sleep won't solve. I probably need some sugar in my system as well."

Grandma and Ava walked into the living room. "Are you boys planning on helping bake these cookies?" Grandma asked, a neon pink apron tied around her waist.

Ava grabbed Mr. Wombington from the floor and said, "Even he's going to help."

"Wow, Mr. Wombington is very dedicated," Grandpa said with a clap.

My mind wandered, trying to make sense of the strange sight I witnessed.

"Enzo, I think you need to eat," Grandma said. "You're as pale as a ghost."

"You're right, Grams. How long until those cookies are done?"

"Only helpers get to eat." Ava put her hands on her waste, Mr Wombinton's long legs draping on the floor.

"Fine, fine." Grandpa stood up.

"Good," Grandma said, returning to the kitchen, Ava at her heels.

"Are you coming?" Grandpa asked.

"In a minute," I replied. "I need to get something from my bag in my room."

"Sounds good." He retrieved to the kitchen.

I rushed up the stairs, determined to find any clues pointing to the creature I'd seen.

I scanned the wall covered in family portraits, but aside from baby pictures of Ava and I, there was nothing unusual.

I found my bag next to a bookshelf inside the room. I put my phone on the nightstand and gazed outside the window, the streaks of orange and purple across the sky an invitation for me to forget everything else for a minute and appreciate the view. But the image of the dull gray eyes haunted me.

"Prince," I whispered. "It called me prince."

I stayed rooted to my spot until the last glimpse of the sun was drowned by the rolling dark clouds.

Ava knelt on top of a stool, elbows resting on the marble countertop.

"There you are," Grandma said once I walked in the kitchen.

"We thought you decided to run away." Grandpa laid a few cookies on a tray. "What did you need to get in your room that took you so long?"

"I thought I packed this book, but it wasn't in my bag." I shrugged. "Guess I left it back home." I reclined on the countertop next to Ava, watching her carefully organize the cookies on her tray into a line. "These look great. Are they for me?"

She scoffed. "These are for Mr. Wombington. He said he's hungry."

On the other side of the large glass doors of the kitchen, in the center of the backyard, was the tree that gave me goosebumps when I was younger. Even in the summer, the tree would grow no leaves, its trunk always gray and old. Its branches reminded me of the drawings of rivers on maps. I remember seeing the eerie tree always decorated with lights. This year was no different.

"The tree still scares you?" Grandma put a tray of cookies in the oven.

"It used to. I just find it creepy. It's just there, taking up space. Aside from being used as a hanger for more Christmas lights every year, what else do you need it for? And it looks so old."

"Oh, I see." Grandma scoffed and put a hand on her waist. "So everything that looks old must be cut down?" A frown followed.

"You know what I mean."

"Regardless of its appearance, it still serves a purpose." She opened the refrigerator and grabbed a bowl of cookie dough, placing it on the counter. "Remember, the value of something isn't lost because its appearance is old. It's the heart that's the most precious treasure of all."

"So that tree has a heart?" I folded my arms over the counter and rested my chin on my hands.

"All things do," she replied, looking as if I should've known the answer to my question. "And they beat in different rhythms, but one needs a good ear to listen."

"Are you drunk on eggnog already?" I pouted my lips.

"Excuse me?" Grandma widened her eyes. "I haven't had eggnog in years."

"Can I have some eggnog?" Ava asked.

"You most certainly cannot," Grandpa replied. "What made you think…"

Their voices turned to muffled sounds, my attention returning to the tree. The Christmas lights bounced as its branches moved to the wind. The sight gave me a mixture of peace and curiosity as the first snowflakes started falling, the sky a shade of dark pink and gray.

We sat by the counter as the cookies baked. My grandparents decided to entertain Ava's imaginary tales about her adventures with Mr. Wombington. I smiled and nodded occasionally, still haunted by the image of the eyes by the stairs.

By the times the cookies were done, the backyard was covered in a blanket of snow. The wind picked up, the moving branches of the tree now looking more like illuminated waving hands.

"Let me just fix us some hot cocoa." Grandma stared at the three cookie trays on the counter with great pride.

A phone vibrated.

"Oh, that must be mine." Grandma had left her phone on top of the microwave. "Your father is saying you haven't replied to his texts, Enzo."

"Phone's off and it's also upstairs." I shrugged and used my foot to spin the stool I was sitting on. "I want a vacation from everything and everyone."

"Do you have a phone, Ava?" Grandma asked while typing.

"Not really. My tablet has VideoTube for kids and that's about it." She used her hands to support her face, elbows on the counter. "I want cookies!"

"Kids are hungry, Mary." Grandpa walked to the large glass door, hands in his pockets. "Tell Bane kids are okay and we'll send news tomorrow."

He stood as still as a statue, watching the storm.

"What are you looking at, Grandpa?" Ava asked.

"The snow," he replied. "It calms me down."

"Your grandpa loves watching a snowstorm." Grandma put the phone on the counter, screen facing down.

"Why?" Ava made use of her foot to turn the stool so she could face him.

"It reminds me of a simpler time." A long breath followed his words.

"A time when he had less wrinkles and his hair wasn't so gray," Grandma said, opening the cabinet and grabbing four white mugs.

"Well, that too." He chuckled. "When I was your age, Enzo, I'd watch every storm. I remember thinking, *'Another snowfall. Another winter. Another day closer to being an adult.'* I wish I had spent less time thinking of the future when I was younger. But things were different then."

"Way to bum everyone out on Christmas eve, Nicholas," Grandma said, a hand on her waist. "Now enough of this." She waved us away. "Cookies are done. Hot cocoa is ready. Go to the living room and I'll serve you all."

"Need help, Grandma?" Ava slid down the stool, Mr. Wombington in her arms.

"No need to help, sweetheart," Grandma replied.

The three of us retrieved to the living room. Mr. Wombington's long legs bounced behind Ava as she pranced.

"Which Christmas movie are we watching tonight?" Grandpa asked as Ava jumped on the brown couch facing the television.

"*The Grinch!*" Ava squealed as I sat beside her. "Please, please, please?"

"*The Grinch* it is." He sat on the couch opposite to ours.

"Do I get a vote?" I asked with a shrug.

"Nope," Ava said.

Grandma showed up and placed the tray overflowing with cookies on the coffee table. We went for them like a lion attacking its prey.

The driveway was buried under the snow, a thick layer already settled over the car. A pink hue stretched across the sky, creating a beautiful spectacle behind the trees.

For the duration of the movie, my attention shifted between the stairs and the television. I was determined to find anything that explained what I saw. I wanted to believe the sight was a fruit of my imagination, but my gut told me otherwise. Who did the eyes belong to? What did the voice mean when it called me *prince*?

"One more movie!" Ava demanded when the credits rolled on the TV.

"It's almost eleven." Grandma stood to her feet and rubbed her eyes.

Grandpa repeated her gesture and said, "Tomorrow is Christmas. We have to be up early for presents."

"Presents!" Ava grabbed my arm. "Heard that, Enzo? Presents. As in more than one!"

A smile was my response.

"We should watch *Home Alone*," Ava jumped to her feet, eyes shifting to Grandma and Grandpa. "Can we, please?"

"Won't you be too tired in the morning?" Grandpa asked.

"No, I promise." Ava laced her fingers together and shook her hands as if begging for a miracle.

"Are you staying up with her, Enzo?" Grandpa asked.

"Sure," I replied. "I'll stay with her."

"Well, alright then." Grandpa stretched. "See you in the morning," he said behind a yawn.

Ava and I wished them goodnight as they walked upstairs to their bedroom.

I leapt from the couch and raced toward the fireplace the moment I heard them locking their door.

"What're you doing?" Ava asked, kneeling in front of the TV with the remote in hand, Mr. Wombington beside her.

"Just looking at something." I grabbed the framed drawing and sat on the couch facing the TV.

"Can you find *Home Alone* on this thing?" Ava shrugged, her attention on the bright screen.

"Yeah, in a minute." The tips of my fingers trailed over the frame as the image of the burning drawing flooded my head. Aside from the smudges and a few uncolored outlines, the drawing showed nothing unusual.

"Give me that." Defeated, I tossed the frame on the couch and reached for the remote. "Maybe it was my imagination," I mumbled while scrolling down the on-demand channel.

"Are you okay?" Ava asked. "We can watch something—"

Ava and I were startled by a clash on the window, the glass now covered in cracks.

"What was that?" Ava reached for Mr. Wombington and held him between her arms.

"Probably a branch."

The wind howled like a pack of wolves. A curtain of white blinded the view outside.

A breeze brushed on my cheek. I jumped up, dropping the remote on the couch.

"What's wrong?" Ava asked as I rushed to the foot of the stairs. I scanned the steps, the walls, the ceiling. Nothing unusual.

A knock came from the kitchen. I followed the sound, my gaze meeting the glass door. The ghost of the colorful lights on the eerie tree danced in the middle of the storm. There was a layer of snow pressed against the glass, rising a few feet from the ground.

I stepped into the kitchen, searching the darkness for whatever had caused the noise.

Three knocks echoed behind me.

I turned my attention to the sound. My teeth sunk into my bottom lip as feeling escaped every limb in my body. Something—or someone stood at the foot of the stairs. It had holes for eyes, lips pressed into a long line rising up the side of its face. Around its head were thorn-covered vines twisted into a crown. Its upper body was shielded by a rusty breastplate, its tattered black pants were tucked into dark boots. Its chest lifted with slow breaths before it started making its way up the stairs.

"Ava!" I darted into the living room.

She was nowhere to be seen.

"Grandpa! Grandma! Help!" I shouted, rushing to the stairs, but the sound of the door sliding in the kitchen stole my attention. Ava ran into the storm with Mr. Wombington in hand, wearing her pink slippers, the legs of her pajamas dragging on the ground.

"Ava!" I shouted, putting on a pair of Grandpa's boots that sat by the door. I followed her, the snow almost to my knees. She giggled while flailing her warms in the air, prancing like a kid running at an amusement park.

My breath steamed as I kept on shouting her name, trudging through the fresh layer of snow on the ground. Not once did she look at me.

A human-like silhouette stood by the frightening tree. But its true form didn't remain hidden for long. The Christmas lights bounced off its armor, its crown of thorns visible. It beckoned Ava closer with a wave, a smile on its face. A scar streaked across its nostrils, rising toward its forehead. And behind him, on the bark of the tree was a doorway.

"Ava!" My throat stung as the wind carried my voice away.

A haunting screech came from the house. I halted and followed the hair-raising sound. Something broke through the roof, crawling out like a corpse digging out of its grave.

"You want him?" My attention followed Ava's voice. She held up her teddy bear, the creature grabbing it with its hands.

"Where are you going to take him?" Ava asked as the creature tossed the teddy bear through the doorway on the tree, the toy fading into the darkness.

The being smiled.

"I can come with you?" Ava extended her hand.

"Stop!" I grabbed her by the shoulder and pulled her to me. The creature squawked, revealing a set of jagged yellow teeth, its breath smelling of decay.

"Get away from that thing!" Grandpa stood by the massive door in the kitchen, Grandma at his side, both in their robes. They ventured into the storm, rushing our way.

A roar blared from the roof. A shadow lingered over the shingles, pacing impatiently.

"Ava, we have to get out of here!" I shook her by the shoulder, but she didn't move. Her eyes remained on the being by the tree, hypnotized by the sight.

A roar echoed behind me. Whatever had found its way up on the roof leapt in our direction, landing beside us. The Christmas lights wrapped on the branches of the tree revealed its face as it approached its companion: holes for eyes, a crown of thorns around its head, chest hidden behind a rust-covered breastplate. In its grasp was a throbbing light.

"What do you want?" Grandpa shouted, now a few feet behind us, body and hair covered in snow.

They stood immobile, their long lips pressed into a line, the Christmas lights reflecting on their breastplates.

Grandma trudged closer and wrapped her arms around Ava.

"Don't harm them," Grandpa begged. "Leave them alone. Your business is with me."

"Ava!" Grandma shook her. "Can you hear me?"

No movement. Her eyes remained open, jaw parted, the brown of her hair replaced by a layer of snow.

The creature I had seen on the stairs stretched its hand and unrolled its fingers, revealing an illuminated globe. The object shattered, its shards turning into a whirling cloud that slithered on the ground as if life had found it. It encircled the four of us and engulfed my grandparents. Fear wrapped me as the cloud quickly retrieved toward the creature and made its way into its opened mouth, Grandma and Grandpa nowhere to be seen.

The lights of the house went dark as they disappeared inside the doorway on the tree.

# CHAPTER 6

Ava took in a sharp breath as soon as they were out of sight. She looked left and right, glanced at her trembling hands and then at my face.

"What were you doing?" I asked, the Christmas lights on the tree casting colorful shadows on her face. "Why did you follow that thing? Why wouldn't you stop? Why wouldn't you listen?"

"Enzo, I tried," she whimpered, lips blue. "But I couldn't. It told me to follow and I did. I couldn't stop. I could only look at it."

"So, what, that thing held you against your will?" My teeth chattered as the snow piled on my shoulder.

"I don't know—I was confused—"

"They took your teddy bear. Any idea why?"

"No." Her chin wobbled. "I don't know what's going on."

"Did you see Grandma and Grandpa being taken by that cloud?" I shuddered.

"I did," she answered with glassy eyes. "I saw everything. I just...couldn't move."

"Let's go inside—maybe call the police," I suggested.

"Maybe?" She frowned.

"What are we going to tell them, Ava?" I shrugged. "That two monsters kidnapped our grandparents?"

Every part of my body trembled as we darted back to the house. My pants were drenched, hair completely covered in ice. Ava had her arms coiled to her chest, teeth chattering like a machine gun.

A layer of snow hid the threshold of the kitchen door, spreading across the floor. I closed the glass door, removed the soaked pair of boots, and went straight to the living room.

Relief found me once I heard the crackling of the fireplace. The house sat in darkness, the fire casting dancing shadows around the living room.

"I'm s-s-s-so cold." Ava removed her wet slippers and stretched her hands over the fire.

I blew into my hands and held them over the flames, my breath still steaming out of my mouth. I followed a cold wind chill that brushed my neck, noticing snow falling on the stairs leading up to the bedrooms. I stared for a while, fear keeping me rooted to my spot.

"Wait here," I said, finally deciding to break free from its sudden hold.

"Enzo, where-where-are you going?" She whimpered.

"I need to make sure there's no one else in here." My eyes shifted between her and the stairs. "Stay here."

I rushed back to the kitchen and grabbed the soaking wet boots I had worn to chase Ava. To my relief, the lights of the house turned back on. I quickly glanced at the glass door, shuddering at the distant twinkling lights, visible even through the storm.

I retrieved to the stairs, the wooden floor creaking to my steps. Pieces of wood and shingles were strewn on the steps, the sight covered in a thin blanket of snow. As I walked up, my gaze shifted to the hole on the ceiling, the night sky in view. Glass crunched beneath my feet as I continued up the steps.

"Enzo, are you alright?" Ava shouted.

"All good!"

The door of my grandparents' bedroom was to my left, wide open, pillows and comforter on the floor. I rushed up the remaining steps, jumping over wood and ice, darting into the room.

Shards of glass were dispersed on the carpet. A cold breeze blew through the half-opened window. I tossed the pillows and the comforter back on the bed, searching for any clues pointing to their captors. But there was nothing. I checked their phones on their nightstand. No signal.

Disbelief took me as I sat on the edge of the bed.

"Damn it." The room blurred behind my welling tears. "Damn it. Damn it." My gaze shifted to the ground, elbows on my knees. In front of me was a piece of parchment paper, its edges jagged.

"Henderbell," I mouthed the strange word written in black ornamental letters. "Henderbell," I repeated, picking it up.

I folded the parchment, tucked it in my pocket, and went into my bedroom to retrieve my phone. There was also no signal. Disappointed, I dropped it back on the nightstand and rushed downstairs.

"Anything?" Ava asked the moment I was in view, hands still stretched over the fire.

"Nothing," I replied. "And none of the phones are working."

She sat on the couch and grabbed a pillow, holding it between her arms. "We can't just leave them. Who knows where they took them?"

"We'll think of something." My attention shifted to the Christmas tree, my mind scurrying to find a way to fight against the nightmare this night had become.

"Maybe it's us," Ava whispered, the reflection of the fire displayed in her eyes.

"What?"

"There's trouble everywhere we go." She shrugged. "Mom and Dad are always at it when we're around. And now we get here and Grandma and Grandpa are taken by those things. Maybe it's us, Enzo. Maybe we're cursed."

Sorrow gripped me.

"Don't say that." I placed an arm around her shoulder. "Hey, we'll figure this out. This is just fear talking, okay?"

She gave me a nod of agreement, wiping her nose with a wrist.

"And we aren't cursed," I continued, struggling to believe my own words. "We're just in an unfortunate situation. We just have to figure this all out."

Beside her was the frame with my drawing, the object triggering a knot in my throat. I grabbed it from the couch and placed it on my lap, the lights of the tree reflected on the glass.

My brows furrowed at the sight of a speckle of light glistening on the paper's surface.

I quickly jumped to my feet and unscrewed the frame, picking up the paper by its edges. More speckles of light were in view, moving around the paper's surface, crawling to the opposite side of the paper likes ants.

"What's wrong?" Ava stood up, alarmed. "Did you see anything else?"

I held the paper by the fire and flipped it. It was as if the flames in the fireplace had the power to order the glimmering moving dots to trace another drawing. "Do you see it?"

"I do," she replied. "Do you think it means something?

The picture depicted the same tree from the backyard, sketched in golden lines, the ground drawn with charcoal. There were four red handprints on its bark and the word *Henderbell* written between them. I tucked a hand in my pocket, feeling the strange note inside.

"Come with me." I ran to the stairs, drawing in hand.

"What? Where?" she asked, grabbing Grandma's bright blue slippers from under the couch.

"I think I know a way to find the door again." I ran up a few steps, treading through the snow-covered rubble from the roof. "Careful with all this stuff on the floor," I said, glancing back at her, snow piling on my shoulders.

She stood at the foot of the stairs, staring as if watching a horror movie.

"Tell you what," I said. "You walk ahead of me. I'll go behind you to make sure nothing sneaks up on you."

"Okay," she mumbled, her breath steaming out of her mouth.

She leapt over the pieces of wood, avoiding the scattered shards of glass as she made her way up.

"Hey," I said once the both of us were up the last step, "go put on some warm clothes."

"Where are we going?" A frown found her face.

"Into the storm," I replied.

"What, we're going back out there?"

"You have to trust me." I showed her the drawing. "We have to touch it. See? It's the tree from the backyard. The four hands on the bark—well, maybe those are our hands. Maybe that's how we'll find the door again. This could be a clue."

"Enzo, even I've seen enough movies to know this could be a trap." She scrunched her face.

"I mean, what other clues do we have? What else can we do? And after seeing those things—" I winced at the haunting memory of the creatures "—who knows what else we're going to find. And they did walk through a door on the tree. You saw that, right?"

"I did," she replied, her face displaying her inner battle with her thoughts.

"This could be it," I said. "Trust me."

She nibbled on the corner of her lips and whispered, "Okay."

I folded the drawing, tucked it in my pocket, and walked into my room. I grabbed the only heavy hooded jacket I brought. It was blue and had two pockets. I put on my snow boots, a black beanie, my gray gloves, and rushed out.

Ava had on a bright pink coat, yellow snow boots, blue gloves, and a white beanie over her head.

"Are you afraid of what we might find on the other side of the door?" she asked once we were at the foot of the stairs.

"I'm more afraid of not finding our grandparents." A shudder followed.

"Well, at least now we know magic is real," she mentioned as we entered the kitchen, most of the snow melted over the threshold.

"Maybe not the best way to find out," I retorted.

"At least we did." Her lips pressed into a line.

Fear gripped me at the image of the tree, the Christmas lights wrapped around its branches bouncing with the wind. My hands reached into my pockets; in one a mysterious parchment, in the other a magical drawing.

Another layer of snow spilled over the kitchen floor once I slid the glass door open. It was as if the tree stared at me, harboring an all-consuming evil. If I was right, I feared what we were going to find on the other side. But an echoing thought whirled deep in my mind. If magic was real, what other stories and imaginings existed?

We stepped under the storm, snow up to our knees.

The wind blew harder, the snow piled with my every breath, and the colorful bouncing lights ahead triggered more questions. Why did the creatures kidnap them and left us behind?

"Alright," I said, the tree in front of me. "On three?" I removed my gloves and wiped away the layer of snow that had settled over the bark.

"Okay," Ava answered with a shudder as she exposed her bare hands.

"One, two, three." My palms touched the rough cold surface. Ava followed my act.

A thin golden line appeared across the bark, drawing the shape of a doorway. We jerked our hands away from the tree and quickly put our gloves back on as vines sprung around the door, acting like hinges.

"No way," Ava said, a reddish hue coming from the Christmas lights reflected on her face.

It was like being inside the most twisted of dreams.
I stepped closer and clutched the bumpy surface, pulling the door open. In front of me was a passageway stretching into the dark.

"Are you ready to do this?" I asked.

"No," she answered. "I've never been around magic. I don't know what to expect."

# CHAPTER 7

The door behind us slammed shut. Darkness and silence settled. The air was damp, the ground moist, and my heart seemed to be competing in a race.

"Enzo?" Ava's voice echoed.

"I'm here."

My hands trembled, Ava's ragged breaths a melody in my ear.

I waited for a source of light to appear—something that could reveal our surroundings, but there was nothing.

Ripples appeared in the darkness, like pebbles thrown on a lake. They stretched above us, forming a dome, our reflections now on display before us. The darkness thinned like drifting fog, the unseen slowly replaced by a wintery forest. My boots were buried in snow, my breath steam. In front of me were tall trees, their branches drooping down due to the snow clinging to them. Streaks of purple and orange painted the sky.

"Holy crap." Behind was the eerie tree from the backyard—the doorway nowhere to be seen, the Christmas lights gone.

"Where do you think we are?" Ava's breath was smoke.

"It's not like I've been here before." Fear was replaced by curiosity. Did I rejoice at the world I found inside a tree? Did I revel in the fact that magic was real?

The sound of fluttering wings traveled through the air. From the woods emerged winged creatures, flying in our direction. I blinked several times as they drew closer, making sure my eyes weren't playing tricks.

"Do you see them?" Ava asked.

"You bet I do."

Their brown wings were like a moth's, full of patterns and lines. They resembled tiny humans, only they had no eyes, nostrils, or lips. Their faces were smooth and empty. They ignored our presence as they flew by, darting toward the sky.

"Were those…fairies?" Ava asked, observing the now distant dots.

"Impossible." My heart raced. "You think that's what those were?"

"I don't know about you, but I've never seen butterflies that look like that back home."

"Well," I scratched my head, "we did just find a door on a tree."

She chuckled, surveying our surroundings as if trying to find reason.

The chiming of bells cut through the air, growing louder with my every breath. A jolt of adrenaline shot through my body as Ava and I backed into each other, my eyes searching for the source of the sound.

Hovering snowflakes appeared from the woods. They followed the wind, organized like a flock of birds. The strange sight quickly approached us, coming to a halt just a few inches away. They spun in the air and formed the shape of a human face.

"Who are you?" demanded a croaked voice.

Reason left me. Did I reply? Did I try to engage in conversation?

"Can you talk?" it insisted after my brief silence.

"What…are…you?" I asked.

"Don't talk to it." Ava pulled on my jacket. "We don't know what it is."

"*It?*" The hovering particles of ice formed a frown. "I have a name. Doopar."

The snowflakes melted, forming the shape of a girl while dripping on the ground. First appeared brown boots covered in mud, then a purple coat draping to the knees. A red scabbard clung to the black belt around her waist. A shudder escaped my lips when her purple eyes appeared. Pointy ears stuck out from her braided fair hair, the back dropping to her waist.

"She looks like one of those action figures you used to have from that medieval game you liked," Ava mentioned.

My cheeks flushed.

"What is medieval?" Doopar pulled her brows together. She stared like we were a bunch of poisonous insects about to sting her. "Is that a weapon? How do you play this game? Who are you?"

"No, no," I said. "Medieval like the time period. When people lived in castles and—"

"People still live in castles. I'm not sure what you mean." Her fingers laced the hilt of her sword. "Who are you?"

"There's no need—"

A gasp replaced my words as she unsheathed her weapon, its tip pointed at us.

"Maybe this will help you answer faster," she said, my heart racing in my chest. "Who are you?"

"Hey, hey, there's no need to point that thing." I threw my hands in the air.

"Then answer the question." She stepped forward. "Who are you?"

"We actually ended up here because our grandparents were kidnapped..." My voice trailed off, certain the story would get Ava and I killed. But then I looked at her and realized madness might actually be embraced in this place.

"Kidnapped and..." She cocked her head. "I'm losing my patience, boy. Are you enemies of Ghenthar?"

"Enemies? No, no. And yes, yes, yes they were kidnapped by two strange beings." My hands clenched into fists. "This cloud came out of a globe and took them. The creatures walked through a doorway on the bark of the tree behind me. It's insane, I know, but—"

"What did they look like?" She seemed alarmed at my words. "These beings you speak of?"

"Tall, no eyes, with thorns around their heads," I replied. "Please, don't kill us. It's the truth. I swear."

"So you've seen the Shadow Spirits." She frowned. "How did you get here? Are you from across the ocean?"

"Across the ocean...no," Ava said, the palm of her hands facing her. "There was a door on the tree and that's how we got here. Please don't kill us. They also have my best friend."

"You came from the other side of that tree?" Doopar's right eyebrow arched up, her posture stiffening.

"Yes." My hands trembled. "And then we saw these fairies flying from the woods."

"What are fairies?" Doopar asked.

"I don't know what you call them." I shrugged, hoping my words had the power to disarm her. "They had wings. They were flying. They looked like tiny people on wings."

"Do you mean neomers?" If her eyes could speak, they'd probably tell me how insane I sounded.

"Sure," I said. "Neomers. We saw them and then you showed up. I swear."

I let out a sigh of relief when Doopar sheathed the sword back into its scabbard. "What are your names?"

"Enzo and this is Ava."

A frown followed our answer. "Is this your first time in Henderbell?" She rested her hands on her waist.

"Yes—I mean, yes." I struggled to find words to answer. Her beauty was enchanting and intimidating. "It's...it's also the first time we've heard of it. I found these—" I quickly retrieved the parchment and drawing from inside my pocket "—at my grandparents' house before walking through the door on the tree."

The objects received a confused stare. "And you've never heard of Henderbell until now?" she asked.

"No," I replied.

"I've seen this handwriting before." She grabbed the parchment from my hand with a scowl. An uncomfortable silence lingered as she analyzed it. "And that?" She cocked her head at the drawing, handing the parchment back to me.

"I drew the picture on one side. I'm not sure who drew the picture on the other," I said, folding the parchment, putting it back in my pocket.

"I'm also familiar with that drawing," Doopar revealed. "Someone gave it to me a long time ago."

"So, what, this drawing belongs to you?" I asked.

"One of them does," she answered. "I'm not sure why it made its way to you. But that doesn't matter. The man who gave me the drawing left a long time ago."

"Left and went where?" The drawing joined the parchment in my pocket.

"Albernaith, your world. Earth, as you call it." Her purple eyes shimmered like precious stones.

"Who taught you how to use a sword?" Ava's gaze was fixed on Doopar's weapon.

"My father," Doopar replied. "He said all girls needed to learn how to kill their enemies with a blade. It took him a while to come to terms with the fact his little girl wanted to join the elven guard of Henderbell, but once he did, he helped me hone my fighting skills. He was an amazing warrior."

"I like that." Ava was transfixed by the sword. "Can I touch it?"

"Ava." I grabbed her arm. "Are you—"

"There's nothing wrong with a woman holding a blade." Doopar unsheathed the weapon. Its handle was maroon, with two antlers rising from the bottom.

I released Ava from my grip.

"Be really careful." She beckoned Ava closer with a wave. "It's very sharp."

Ava touched the handle, her face reflected on the silver blade.

"It's beautiful," she said.

Her eyes shifted between my sister and me, a smirk on her lips. "I should take you to the castle before nightfall. It'll be safer for everyone. And since you have that drawing and that parchment, I have no choice but to believe you are who you say you are, but someone in the castle will know better than I."

"And who are we again?" I asked.

"Just two humans lost in Henderbell." Doopar tilted her head to the side. "That's all you are, right? There's nothing else to your story?"

"We aren't lying, if that's what you're implying," I contested.

"I believe you," Doopar affirmed. "But like I said, someone in the castle will know better."

"What if you're the one lying?" I pointed a finger at her. "What if you're an enemy or something?"

She scoffed. "If this is your first time in Henderbell, then you shouldn't be worried about having enemies here, correct?"

"I guess." I shrugged.

"If I turn out to be one, you're free to stay here in the Forest of Nick after nightfall." My cheeks flushed as Doopar approached me, her eyes cut like piercing blades. "Now if you're willing to give me a chance, then you might actually have a decent place to eat and sleep tonight." Her breath brushed my cheeks. She smirked and continued toward the woods.

"I'm going with her." Ava darted in her direction.

"Ava!" I protested. "We don't even know her. And she just had a sword pointed at us."

"I don't want to freeze." Ava halted and spread out her arms. "And exactly, *she* has a sword. We have a better chance of surviving with her. Do you want to hang around in this forest?"

"How can you be so willing to believe her?" I asked.

"She's giving us a chance," Ava replied. "Maybe we should do the same. Let's trust the magic we found."

We trudged through the snow-covered ground as denser purple streaks appeared in the orange sky. All one could hear were our footsteps crushing the soft powder. Doopar walked ahead, glancing over her shoulder every once in a while, ensuring we still followed. Ava stared at Doopar like she'd found a hero. I stared because of her strange power to hold my attention.

"Why do you turn into snow?" I asked, shifting my head away from a branch.

"It's faster to get around," Doopar replied. "I'm not used to moving at a human pace."

"What are you?" Ava asked, her cheeks red from the cold.

"I'm an elf." Her words carried a tone of confusion "I think the ears and the fact I told you I belong to the elven guard gave that away, no?"

"That's so cool. I never met an elf before." Ava's eyes widened. "Where were you born?"

"In Ghenthar, the city we're going, the capital of Henderbell." She leapt over the fallen bark of a tree with incredible agility, landing on the tips of her toes. Ava and I crawled over it like a bunch of buffoons. Our clumsiness earned a chuckle from Doopar.

"Is Ghenthar a nice place?" Ava continued, wiping the snow from her gloves on her pink jacket, which seemed way brighter when surrounded by piles of snow.

"It's all I've ever known. But elves were born across the ocean in Lestee. My father was brought here as a slave years ago, along with my mother. We don't age as fast as humans, so elves were the perfect beings for slave work."

"Are you still a slave?" I asked.

"I was never one. I was born after my kind was liberated. My father and mother served many kings in Henderbell, but died twenty-five years ago."

"I'm sorry," I said, narrowing my eyes at a black two-headed owl cleaning its wings with the beak belonging to its right head.

"It was a long time ago." Her attention remained on the forest. "One hundred human years equals three hundred for an elf. At least they got to see their people free."

"Why are you so eager to help us when you were so skeptical before?" Though I feared the answer to my question, I continued speaking. "You only just found us."

"Going by the clothes you're wearing and the objects you're carrying, I can tell you aren't from here, and it's not in my nature to leave people to freeze to their deaths," she replied. "So I'd much rather take you to the castle and learn more about where you're from before making any further judgement."

"What's wrong with our clothes?" Ava looked down and scanned her jacket.

"No one dresses like that in Ghenthar or anywhere else in this world," Doopar answered with a grin.

The rays of the sun broke through the canopy of trees ahead, its light reflected on icicles hanging from a few of the branches. We walked past the vegetation, emerging in front of a cliff. A vast winter forest was on full display below, stretching up the mountains on the horizon, their peaks covered in a blanket of snow. Birds flew across the purple and orange sky, some releasing glowing particles as they flapped their wings. A river snaked through the valley, where it encircled a city protected by walls

"Wow," Ava said, eyes bulging out of their sockets.

"What you see before you is the Forest of Nohein." She pointed at the city. "And that is the city of Ghenthar."

"So what exactly is Henderbell?" I asked while absorbing the beauty of the landscape.

"This is the country of Henderbell, made up of twelve kingdoms. Their rulers answer to our king and queen, who live in a castle in the city," Doopar answered.

"You have a king and a queen?" Ava's words carried excitement.

"Yes," Doopar chuckled, "though at times I wish we didn't."

A rustling sound came from the trees. Purple birds scattered from the trees. A frill of scarlet feathers surrounded their heads, their eyes white. Trails of light streaked behind them as they flew away.

"This is unreal," I mumbled. "It's like I'm in a dream or something. I wish Billy and Cliff could see me now."

The valley and its beauty made me certain this was no dream. I could never make this up. Even in my wildest imaginings, I had never created something so majestic.

"How do we get to the castle?" Ava asked. "Do we have to walk all the way?"

Doopar shrugged while taking in a breath, her golden hair following a gentle breeze. "I've had enough walking for a day." She stretched her hand. "Place both of your hands here."

Ava and I followed her command. My skin was covered in thin white lines, which spread out like spiderwebs. A cold chill wrapped my entire body as a layer of ice engulfed me. My body shattered in the air like glass, only instead of shards, the broken pieces were snowflakes. I could still see, but everything around me went quiet.

We plunged down the cliff, making our way through the forest; my stomach—or whatever it was at that moment—rising to my throat. There were bears with horns, strange birds, squirrels with wings, and many other creatures that barely resembled anything I had ever seen.

So this was it.

This is what magic felt like.

# CHAPTER 8

Doopar's magic released me once we reached the edge of the forest. Ahead was a massive golden gate, its bars wrapped in vines laden with red roses. Beside the gate was a gray stone wall extending beyond sight.

"That was great!" Ava squealed. "Can I be an ice princess?"

Doopar smiled. "You can be anything you want, Ava."

"You're incredible," I said, instantly regretting my compliment.

Doopar tilted her head. "That's the wisest thing you've said ever since you got here."

My cheeks flushed as she walked out of the vegetation, heading in the direction of the gate.

"Somebody has a crush," Ava whispered, nudging me on the rib.

"Can you blame me?" I scoffed.

"Coming?" Doopar shouted, glancing over her shoulder.

We followed her. Soldiers patrolled the wall walk, their armors glistening with their every move. Antlers clung to the side of their helmets, rising above their heads.

"Are those the good guys?" Ava asked as we got closer.

"That depends on whose side you're on," Doopar answered. "Since they know me, we should be alright."

"What kind of answer was that?" I asked, the snow crunching at my every step.

"The truth." Doopar frowned. "There's no good or evil. Just perspective, Enzo. It'll do you well to remember that."

We halted a few feet away from the gate.

"Now what?" My eyes were locked on the guards patrolling the wall. They stood still, watching us as if we were rabid dogs.

Doopar seemed nervous.

"Is everything okay?" Ava asked.

"Yes," Doopar replied quickly. "Everything is fine."

Silence hovered for a few seconds, broken by Doopar's sigh of relief. The vines slithered across the gate. Rose petals scattered in the air as the golden doors creaked open.

"Well," she said with a smile, "it gives me great pleasure to welcome you both to Ghenthar." She gestured the way with her hand.

"You looked worried for a second there," I said as we walked through the gate.

"I thought they were going to give us a hard time," she mentioned.

"Why?" I asked.

"I may be a part of the elven guard, but women who fight are still not that well received in this world." Her face grew rigid. "And some men who think they own reason like to be difficult."

The sudden sorrow that took her eyes was enough for me get a sense of the past lingering behind her greatness.

"Who opened the gate?" I turned to the gate behind me, the vines covered in roses slithered across the iron surface.

"It opened itself," she replied. "Its magic recognizes friend from foe."

"So why do you need guards on the wall?"

"Even magic can be tricked," she answered.

"Can you turn to snowflakes in here?" I asked, noticing the amount of people crowding the narrow cobblestone street.

"No," she replied, disappointed. "After the law that granted our freedom, we were prohibited to use our magic in the city."

Before me were half-timbered houses with roofs in shades of red, purple, and silver; smoke billowed from a few of the chimneys, the smell of bread in the air. Pines wrapped in golden lights laid scattered, their branches covered by layers of snow. Those strolling down the street laughed and chattered, wearing long dresses, boots, coats, and a few eccentric hats.

"I can clearly see what you meant about people not dressing like us." Ahead of me was a woman with a hat shaped like a winged cat. Her orange dress was round like a tea cup, her gloves covered half of her arms, their texture reminiscent of cat hair.

"I already love this place." Ava's eyes were wide, her mouth parted open. "It's so interesting."

"Everyone is getting ready for Christmas," Doopar said. "Christmas is the most important celebration in Henderbell. Henderbellians celebrate their freedom and their god, Kurah."

There were tents where people sold bread, fruits, vegetables, and sweets. Carriages were pulled by blue horses, and with each movement the animals made, sparks of golden light lifted from their coats. I felt a rush when I spotted more elves in the crowd. One would think Doopar would receive honor from her kind, but they frowned and scowled. Some even ignored her outright. I noticed the sight bothered her.

"Enzo!" Ava ran to one of the tents. "Look, look! It's the ornament from the tree! They have one just like it."

I followed her, eyes on the scarlet fabric of the tent. It was bedazzled with gems and rhinestones of many colors, supported by long wooden sticks.

"Look." She pointed at the ornament shaped like an H with antlers. "Isn't it cool?"

"It is." I leaned closer, my reflection displayed on its glass surface.

"You like that one, huh?" asked the bald man inside the tent. He had a thick accent, and lounged on a wooden chair with a silver mug in hand. His buttoned-down shirt was covered in red and green stripes, his overalls brown with beige swirls on each suspender.

"Is there a meaning behind it?" I asked as he took a sip from his drink. "I've seen this ornament before."

The man spit out whatever liquid was in his mouth, setting the mug on his merchandise table crowded with Christmas ornaments. "What do you mean? You don't know what this symbol is?" He fixed the straps of his overalls over his shoulders, staring as if I had just committed the most heinous of crimes.

Ava and I looked at each other, confused.

"They aren't from here, Barthemeus." Doopar was behind us. "Do forgive them."

"What, don't tell me they're from Lestee? I've had it with those bloody Rainsakens folk. They cross the Crystal Sea and think they own the place. Telling you—"

"Isn't that where you're from?" Doopar hissed.

"I was born there, but do you see me living across the sea?" Barthemeus scoffed. "Even I know better."

"Who's rain-sacking?" Ava asked.

Barthemeus tittered. "Rainsakens," he corrected. "What's your name, little girl?"

"Ava."

"That's a pretty name. Alright, do you," he grabbed the ornament, "know the story of King Oden?"

"Not really," she replied, coiling into herself.

"Ah, I see," he turned to me, "and you?"

"I'm with her on this one."

"Where did you find these kids, Doopar?" He scoffed.

She seemed uncomfortable by his question. "They were lost in the woods. I'm taking them to the castle to see if we can find a way to get them back to their parents." Her brows pulled together.

"Poor kids." Barthemeus looked at us like we were two lost puppies. "Tell you what, do you want the ornament, Ava?"

"No, it's okay," Ava said with a nod. "I don't have any money."

"I insist, little Ava." He picked up the object by its golden string, leaned over the table, and placed it in her hand.

Ava giggled, curling her fingers around it.

"Whenever you're in trouble, hold it tight against your chest." Barthemeus smiled. "Help always comes to those who believe"

"Okay." Ava's cheeks flushed. "Thank you."

"Well, I hope you find your parents." Barthemeus smiled. "Let it be in Henderbell as it is in your heart."

"Same to you," said Doopar.

Ava waved the man goodbye, holding the ornament.

We continued walking through the crowded streets, everywhere something new to see. People sold jewels of all colors and shapes, merchants with tables full of fruits I had never tasted or seen. It was like being in a dream full of magic and wonder. But the sight of the elves frowning at Doopar shattered my temporary fantasy. The elves were regal, walking with their heads high and chests out. Most of them wore cloaks of dark colors that draped to their ankles. Though their hair differed between blond, silver, and white—every single one had purple eyes.

"Why are they looking at you like that?" I asked, heat flushing through my body. "Has no one ever told them not to stare?"

"When you become the first elven woman to join the elven army of Henderbell, you're bound to make some heads turn." Her words carried pride and sorrow. "Even after the elves were granted freedom, some traditions remained. In our culture, women are only meant to care for the house and the children. None have any perspective of adventure or courage. Let the men have exciting lives. Little elven girls aren't encouraged to dream, only to live. Growing up, I'd always tell my dad that life wasn't for me."

"I'm sorry to hear," I said.

"It all worked out in the end." She smiled. "I'm exactly where I want to be."

"Did you ever try to change to fit in with the rest of your kind?" Ava asked, fixing her beanie.

"At some point you try to grow wings even if you're meant to be a lion. And then life teaches you that you are who you are."

"Just like us," Ava added with a smirk, apparently proud to find something in common with Doopar.

My eyes met hers. "What do you mean, Ava?" I was surprised by her comment.

"No one ever told us of this world," she replied, looking at me as if the answer to my question was pretty logical. "But that didn't stop life from catching up with us. Now here we are."

"Where's my sister and what have you done with her?" I asked.

We continued on, parading through the streets until coming to a tall brick wall with wooden spikes at the top. An iron gate was ahead, guarded by armored soldiers.

"Doopar, shouldn't you be cooking for your husband or something?" said one of the guards in a thick accent as he approached us, half of his face hidden behind a helmet shaped like an elk's head. "Oh, wait, you don't have one." He leaned on his spear.

"I don't have time for this, Kormak," she said as his companions laughed. "I need to see Ishmael. Just let me in."

"I bet she plays with all the men in the elven army," said a soldier with a scar running from the tip of his nose to the corner of his right eye. "Will you play with us?" His tongue caressed his chapped lips.

"Just let me in," Doopar insisted, the veins on her neck visible.

"Who are they?" The soldier with the scar insisted, pointing his spear at us. "Never seen their kind in these parts. Are they from Lestee?"

"What's your problem?" My hand curled into fist as I stepped forward.

"Enzo, don't." Ava held me by my wrist.

"What do we have here?" Kormak laughed. "He seems brave. A great fit to protect you, Doopar. Going for the younger type now?"

"At least I know how to treat another human being," I barked, my pulse pounding in my ears.

"A human being?" Laughter erupted from the soldier with the scar. "You aren't from here, are you?"

My body tensed at the snide tone of his question.

"Kid," Kormak started. "Elves aren't human beings. They are *just* beings. And to answer your question, our problem is an elf bringing two strangers into the castle. Not sure who you are, but I've never seen anyone dressed like you." The stench of his breath traveled up my nose. "Never trusted elves. Still don't. And you and the king's advisor may be friendly toward one another, but we still don't trust you." His eyes met Doopar. "Especially now when we also think that Ishmael is sneaking around with an elven boy."

"That's not my problem," Doopar admonished. "Just let me in."

"Only if you play with me as well." Kormak grabbed her arm and puckered his lips.

She jerked away from his grasp, ensnared his other arm, twisted his wrist and pulled him closer, noses inches away from each other. "I was going to take the high road, but if you don't let me in, I'll tell your wife you've been sneaking around with that eighteen-year-old peasant boy. I'll tell her you like to play a different game every once in a while—one that involves a boy as old as your own son."

The soldier's chest rose with quick breaths as wrinkles carved on his forehead. He stared with parted lips, the muscles of his face trembling.

"Do we have a deal?" she asked. The soldier cringed as she twisted his arm a little more. "It's either a deal or a broken wrist."

"Yes, yes!" he shouted.

One of the soldiers rushed our way, spear pointed at Doopar. "You little b—"

"Let her be, Tennar!" begged Kormak as Doopar released him.

Ava observed, face pale.

"You call yourselves guards?" I snapped. "Is it a common thing for you to behave like that in front of a nine-year-old girl?"

"If you ever go to war, boy, you'll find your answer," Kormak replied through gritted teeth while rubbing his wrist.

In front of me was a moat over a lagoon. It led to a golden-brown door, the same color used for the shingles on the roof of the four main towers of the castle—which rose hundreds of feet into the air. Its structure was of bricks, their colors reminding me of chestnuts.

Doopar walked ahead, Ava and I at her heels.

After a while, Ava ran so she could walk beside Doopar. "Sorry those men were so mean to you."

"I'm used to it," Doopar said.

"You shouldn't be!" I declared, rushing my pace. "It takes great courage to be the first to do anything new. People just don't understand that sometimes."

Doopar halted at my words and turned her head to face me. Her lavender eyes met my gaze, sending shudders through my body. She gave me a half-hearted smile and said, "I appreciate your kind words, but they won't change anything."

"Don't let those bad men get you down." Ava held her hand. "It'll be okay. You'll see."

"Thank you," she said with a sigh.

Her words earned a smile from Ava, but my sister's attention was quickly stolen by a flying fish snapping at a few mosquitoes hovering over the water. The creature had wings like a fly, and a snout like a lizard. Soon, many of its kind followed, moving in the air like a well-rehearsed dance piece.

"What are those?" Ava leaned over the wooden rail of the moat.

"They're called mosfish," Doopar answered. "They've existed in Henderbell before any being with a developed conscience. Sometimes, I think they're smarter than any who came to existence after them."

"What do you mean?" I asked.

"Elves and humans are beings with a developed conscience, meaning they possess the ability to rule over land, water, fire, and earth. Their conscience puts them at the top of the survival chain while creatures like the mosfish remained the same throughout time."

"Incredible," I whispered, observing the mosfish as they continued snapping at the mosquitoes. The orange and purple hues of the sunset reflected over the water, creating a spectacle of color. The snow-covered mountains peaked over the wall encircling the moat.

We carried on, coming to the golden-brown door made of wood. Carved on its surface was an elk fighting a dragon with horns all over its snout. At the tip of the stone archway surrounding the door was a symbol shaped like the ornament Barthemeus gave Ava.

"Look!" Ava squealed, removing the ornament from her pocket. "It looks just like it."

"What's that symbol anyway?" I asked.

"The sigil of Henderbell," Doopar replied. "The antlers are a tribute to Kurah, the elk. It was created by King Oden after he defeated Claudius the Fallen."

She grasped the handles on the door and as she was about to pull them, she turned her attention to Ava and me. "Let me do all the talking when we're inside. Ishmael has been on edge since our rulers went missing."

"Alright," I said with a frown.

"Is he like one of those soldiers back there?" Ava asked.

"Not at all," Doopar answered with a scowl. "But he can be a bit stubborn."

# ISHJMAEL

# CHAPTER 9

I chose to seek solitude and silence in the Room of Secrets since the disappearance of King Nicholas and Queen Mary three days ago. Somehow, their captors had found a way into the castle, leaving a pouch made of elk skin on each of their thrones. Inside were locks of their hair and a note. Each piece of paper was sealed with a stamp shaped like a forbidden sigil: a skull with a crown of thorns.

We thought the letters were an attempt to frighten us, until their absence lasted longer than usual. It was customary for them to leave Ghenthar to spend some time in the human realm of Albernaith around Christmas, but never without news.

When their son, Bane Griffin, lived in the castle with me, we used to call this room our fortress. Though I had many fond memories in this place, the past few days exchanged them for fear and uncertainty.

I spent the majority of my time sitting on the same chair, the table in front of me overflowing with books and maps. I read and looked at each one repeatedly, trying to find clues as to how the Shadow Spirits returned and where they could have taken our rulers.

Next to me were the bags left in the throne room. I reached for them, the texture of the fur grazing the palm of my hands sent shivers down my body. I grabbed one of the letters and unrolled it on the table.

*The prophecy of the empty thrones will come to pass.*
*The magic of time is no longer contained in royal blood.*
*We ventured into the human realm and found them.*
*The spirits you once cast away have now returned*
*to avenge who they are.*

*We're not alone.*

Each letter was written in blood. I rolled the paper and put it back on the pouch. On the wall in front of me, hanging by the door was the map of Henderbell, its right edge missing. King Nicholas brought me into this room the day he ripped it. I asked him why he desecrated one of our ancient treasures. His response was that it was simply needed.

I rotated my seat, my gaze shifting to the tall glass window behind me, the horizon painted in shades of purple and orange as the sun set behind the mountains. The people below were like ants walking the streets, oblivious to the fact their rulers were missing, and that an impending doom loomed over them. My face and clothes reflected over the glass, the sunlight causing a glare over the silver pin on my chest shaped like the Henderbellian sigil; my deep purple garments a reminder of how much the king trusted me— a gift given to me on the day he called me to be his advisor. He told me only his advisor wore this shade of purple in the castle as a tribute to their wisdom and faithfulness.

My attention returned to the crowded table, the mess triggering frustration. My elbows rested on the wooden surface, my hands serving as support for my head. Another day gone. Another sunset without any clues on their location.

A knock startled me.

"Come in!" I shouted.

My heart accelerated when he walked in with his silver armor, his purple eyes lighter once struck by the light of the setting sun, his silver hair tied into a tail, a scruff of beard on his face.

"You look dreadful," Loomstak said, sitting in front of me.

"Any news from your elven men?" I asked, hopeful.

"We've scouted the forests and the nearby villages." His hands folded over the table. "I've had elves camped since the day of their disappearance near the river and the Tree of Hender. None have seen or heard anything. No Shadow Spirits were spotted anywhere."

My chest rose with a breath. "So even though I asked to be interrupted only when we had any news, you decided to barge in here for no reason at all."

He smirked. "I think I'm the only one allowed to do such a thing. Besides, I missed looking at those deep brown eyes of yours."

"Maybe Doopar should replace you as commander," I said snidely. "I'm sure she would've found them by now."

He scoffed, clearly displeased at my remark. "I prefer to think that's your exhaustion talking."

"Maybe it is." I released a sigh.

"Is age finally catching up with you?" he smirked.

"I may be thirty-seven, but I bet I could still beat every single elven soldier in you army," I said, finger pointed at him.

He chuckled and touched my arm. "Have you been cooped up in here all day again?"

"I've been going over old scriptures about the Shadow Spirits. Their first appearances, their defeat, trying to spot clues as to how they could've broken free from the Prison of Krishmar and found their way into Albernaith."

"Any luck?" Our eyes locked.

"None." I laid a hand over his. "I don't know what to do anymore. The only logical explanation would be someone setting them free. But for that, they'd need to know magic— deep magic. At least that's what they implied on the notes they left inside those pouches." I pointed at the objects. "But who knows? Maybe they're bluffing. Maybe they're not."

"We'll find them," he said, our fingers lacing together. "But you overburdening yourself won't bring them back."

"Where's Doopar, by the way?" I asked. "Have you heard from her?"

He released my hand. "I asked her to patrol the Tree of Hender. I haven't heard from her yet. I'm sure she would've come to me if she had any news to share."

"Is she alone?" My right eyebrow turned into an arch.

"I hate when you do that with your eyebrow." He leaned back on the chair, running his hand across the top of his silver hair.

"I know you're giving me a half answer. You wanted her away from the rest of your elven men because she's a woman." I sighed. "Respect her. She didn't join your army as a favor. She joined because of merit and honor."

He looked displeased at my words. "Maybe she joined because you've been friends for years."

"Don't be jealous."

He let out a sigh of frustration. "Elven women stay home. They don't fight. And during Christmastime, they don't go wandering with the elven men. They cook and prepare meals. I sent her to the safest place she could be."

"Is that Henderbellian law for elven women?"

He frowned. "No, but have you noticed how people stare at her? It's like she's a poisonous insect."

"Then elven women can do as they wish," I affirmed. "And as far as the staring, I'm sure I can suggest a law of decapitation. People can't stare without their heads."

"Of course." Loomstak's complexion grew rigid. "If only you had the courage to suggest a law that actually mattered, like one allowing the elves to love whomever our hearts longed for." His glistening lavender eyes set my heart racing.

"That's different." I buried my face in the palm of my hands. "And I don't see how this is the best time to discuss such things."

"I don't see the difference," he retorted. "If elven women can now join armies, then my kind should also be allowed to be with human or elf."

"Please, don't do this," I begged. "Not now."

"Don't take this the wrong way," he continued. "I don't mean to take the attention away from our secret crisis. I'm just confused."

"I wish I had all the answers, my love." My gaze lowered to the books in front of me. I didn't need to look at him to see the sorrow in his eyes.

"I wish you'd fight harder," he whispered. "I wish you'd trust more."

"I wish the same," I added. "But sometimes, my hands are tied by powers much stronger than my abilities."

"And yet you wear the clothes of a king's advisor. The only power above yours is the king's." Anger flooded every part of my body. "Remember what King Nicholas said before the entire court when he gave you that pin?" My attention lifted to him, eyes fuming. *"Ishmael Bartowmell, you're to be my advisor in times of war and despair. This pin is a reminder of your wisdom and your ability—"*

*"To turn chaos into peace,"* I finished the sentence with an edge to my voice. "You don't need to remind me. Those words haunt me every single day." I jumped to my feet and walked to the window behind me. "How do you think I feel, Loomstak? Our rulers disappeared after leaving me in charge. The Shadow Spirits—the very enemy my parents died to destroy—have returned under *my* watch. I'm asking you to see this situation through my eyes for a minute."

My reflection displayed on the glass. My hair, once tied into a bun, was now chestnut wisps falling beside my ears.

"I have!" he barked. "Many times in the past few years. All I'm asking is for you to fight for us as much as you fight for the king and queen."

"I owe them," I whispered. "They saved me."

He pushed his chair away from the table, walked up to me and wrapped his arms around my waist, pulling me closer. "I may be unfair with my words, but there's truth to them," he whispered in my ear, the reflection of his eyes glistening on the window. "All I ask is that you fight for our love." I watched the people on the streets as he spoke.

"You see them?" My hand pressed on the glass. "Every single one may die if they aren't on their thrones by Christmas. I think finding them is more important than a law allowing us to display our love in public."

He pulled away. "I guess that's the difference between us." I turned to face him. "The fact I have to hide what I feel for you is the same as drinking a slow-killing poison."

"And if we don't find our king and queen, we'll all die a little faster," I said, frustrated. "You know what I feel for you. I don't need a law to express that."

"It's true. I do know how you feel." He curled his hands into fists.

"Don't lay this burden on me. *Not now.* What matters to me more than love at the moment is discovering how the Shadow Spirits found a way into Albernaith. They knew the exact time and location they were going to be at their house. They discovered how to navigate time between both worlds when supposedly such a secret was never shared outside the Griffin family. Who knows where these creatures are?"

His chest raised with a breath. "What are your orders for the elves, my lord?" he asked in a contemptuous tone.

"Don't make this more difficult, please."

"Tell me how my men and I can be of further service," he said, face rigid.

"Search the Prison of Krishmar."

His head jerked back. "We've searched every corner we're allowed to look. You know Henderbellian laws forbid elves to enter the prison." Loomstak's voice was flat. "We scouted the woods near the prison and saw nothing unusual. Send your human guards then."

"Human senses are not as sharp as yours," I mentioned. "That's where the Shadow Spirits were imprisoned. I believe that's where they may be hiding."

"Seems a little convenient that they'd hide in the place that held them prisoners," he mentioned.

"Or it could be the cleverest of plans." I folded my arms.

"So what would you have me do?" His words carried confusion.

"I'm giving you and your elven men permission to go inside the prison," I said, aware of what was to follow my words.

"So you're overruling Henderbellian law based on need?"

"Breaking this law could save this world and Albernaith. I'll deal with our king and queen once they're found."

"I really hope this is exhaustion talking. Again." Loomstak lost his rigid posture.

"No, it's reason," I said, my attention changing to the two pouches on the table. "I can't fail them. I need you to understand that. My parents died at the hands of the Shadow Spirits. Now our rulers have been taken by them under my watch. I can't fail, Loomstak, and I'll do whatever I need to do."

"It isn't your fault." He looked at me with longing eyes, the same eyes that made me fall for him in the first place. "Their son, Bane, chose to leave with that girl, Evelyn. This was *their* responsibility. And you're taking this burden upon yourself. I know you agreed to be his advisor, but there's only so much a man from Lestee can do here."

"I may be from the land in the east, just like you, but I'm the closest thing King Nicholas and Queen Mary have to family in Henderbell." I took his hands between my own. "I have to honor them in everything I do, including whom I love. Please understand that."

"None in this entire kingdom have proven to be more faithful than you," he started. "You took upon your shoulders a burden that wasn't yours to bear. You told me they have grandchildren in Albernaith too young and unskilled to rule— an offspring none in this kingdom know about. He has too many shadows behind him." He held my face between his hands. "Even the most faithful can't see inside a wicked heart. It'll do you good to remember that."

"So please be faithful and enter the Prison of Krishmar."

His hands dropped to the side of his body.

"I highly doubt the Shadow Spirits will have chosen to hide in there," he said with a nod of disapproval. "But I'll be faithful one more time."

"I'm doing everything I can to change the laws I find unfit for our kingdom." I pulled him closer by his armored wrist.

He made no effort to hide the sorrow on his face. He jerked his wrist away and rushed toward the door.

"Loomstak, please…" He slammed the door shut before I could finish.

I sat on the edge of the table, the map of Henderbell before me. The sight sparked fear that I would fail this world, fear that I'd fail those who took me as their own after the death of my parents when I was twelve.

The memory of their faces haunted me every once in a while. My father's hazel eyes, often surrounded by dark circles; my mother's smile, always persistent regardless of our trials. My father lived as King Nicholas' sorcerer, an honor much too great for my family since we came as settlers from Lestee. Death found him while protecting the castle from the Shadow Spirits twenty-five years ago. My mother lived as a prophetess who failed to see the coming of darkness. I watched her die when they attacked.

A knock on the door startled me.

"Come in!" I shouted, hoping Loomstak would enter the room, but my expectations were defeated when one of the human guards came into view.

"Lord Ishmael, your presence is required in the throne room," said the guard, his face hidden behind the silver helmet with an antler on each side. "Doopar is here with two children found near the Tree of Hender. She claims she needs to speak with you now."

A sinking feeling took my stomach. "Who are these children?"

"She won't say," he replied. "She said she'll answer to you and you alone. That stubborn elf."

My head turned toward the map on the wall. "Tell her I'll be right there."

"At once."

His footsteps faded into silence after he closed the door. My eyes scanned the old map, following the sketches of mountains, rivers, hills, and valleys.

"I won't fail you," I whispered.

# CHAPTER 10

The hall leading to the Room of Secrets was one of my favorite spots when I was younger. Bane and I would wander these parts of the castle, fake swords in hand, pretending we were fighting wars and riding dragons.

Old set of armors had crowded these halls for as long as I could remember. Queen Mary once explained these represented the different designs of Henderbellian armory since King Oden first conquered this side of the sea. On the walls were many weapons: swords, spears, bows and arrows, and above them all, oil paintings depicting Henderbellian wars.

But my favorite spot was the massive stained-glass window shaped like the head of an elk. It pointed west so the last rays of the sun could shine through, filling the hall with a rainbow of colors. Today was no different. A spectacle colored the wall ahead, the scattered rays of light glistening like stars.

I walked down the spiral staircase, greeting the two guards standing by the door leading to the main entrance of the throne room.

The door creaked, revealing the wide hall upheld by white columns that ended on a ceiling covered in paintings depicting warriors in battle. The dark stone platform where both thrones stood was at the end, behind it the white marble statue of Kurah, the elk. Doopar stood at the foot of the platform, two children at her side, and two guards beside them.

"Since when do guards have to follow me into this room?" Doopar asked, hands on her waist.

"It's nice to see you too," I said. "I asked them to accompany anyone who comes into the throne room in the absence of our rulers." I fixed the pin on my chest. "Nothing personal."

The two children watched me as if I were a rare dragon strolling through the forest. Their clothes were unlike anything I had ever seen before. The boy wore what seemed to be a black potato sack, while the girl's pink coat looked like the feathers of a wild bird.

"I think it's best if they leave," Doopar suggested.

"You both may wait outside." I waved both guards away.

On the wall to my left was the swaying silver pendulum, as tall as the columns of this room. It was used to announce the arrival of Christmas in Henderbell. Whenever both worlds aligned, the pendulum stopped moving, standing still for twenty-four hours.

"This place is beautiful," said the young girl, eyes wide.

"Are you going to introduce us, Doopar?" I asked, while the boy stared at me with his nose crinkled into a skeptical scowl.

She chuckled. "Oh, I most certainly will. This is Enzo and Ava Griffin." A smirk followed her words.

Feeling abandoned my limbs. I scanned their faces, immediately finding truth to her words. They had their father's eyes.

"Do you always stare at people like that? It's creepy," Enzo said. "And honestly, it's very uncomfortable."

"I apologize. My name is Ishmael." I took a step back. "I've heard so much about you. I wasn't expecting you both to arrive during such a—" I refrained my words since I didn't know if they knew what had transpired. "Well, I'm glad you're here. Your grandparents always shared so much about you."

"You know our grandparents?" Enzo narrowed his eyes.

I shot Doopar a confused stare. She nodded her head, signaling the children didn't know the information yet.

"So you don't know," I mumbled.

"I figured you should be the one to tell them," Doopar said.

"A few days ago, I called Horthur, the general of our human army, and Loomstak, the commander of our elven troops, to the castle for an urgent meeting where I informed them of our king and queen's disappearance."

"Wait, your king and queen are missing?" Enzo asked.

"Yes," Doopar replied. "Both humans and elves were told to keep the disappearance a secret. Many elves received different assignments; mine was to stay close to the Tree of Hender, since that's how they crossed over to Albernaith, the human world. The threat was taken seriously after two notes were found here in this throne room apparently written by the enemy."

"The Shadow Spirits?" Enzo mumbled, chest heaving.

"Yes," Doopar answered.

"What are…?" Color abandoned Enzo's face. "What are their names?"

"King Nicholas and Queen Mary," I replied.

"Grandma and Grandpa?" Ava shouted, her voice carrying around the room.

"Alright, if I'm understanding this correctly," Enzo cleared his throat, "you're telling us our grandparents, Nicholas and Mary Griffin, are—"

"Are the king and queen of Henderbell." Their jaws dropped at the sound of my words. "Which would make you Prince Enzo and Princess Ava."

Enzo burst into laughter. "Out of all the crazy things I've seen and heard today, this has got to be the most unrealistic of them." He removed his strange hat and ran a hand over his hair. "If we're royalty here, then how come you didn't recognize us instantly?"

"No one is this world has ever seen a picture of you two," I answered. "Few even know your names. They were very secretive about their offspring."

"I'm—I'm no prince." Enzo shrugged, the palm of his hands facing me. "I'm the nerd in school. I'm the guy who didn't grow up. I'm the guy who got dumped by his friends and was cut out of pictures. I'm no royalty. I'm not special."

"Then how did you come across a piece of an ancient Henderbellian map?" Doopar's brows curved upward.

"I don't have a piece of a map…" He reached into his pocket, revealing two pieces of paper: one a drawing I had never seen and another a sight far too familiar.

"I'm afraid Doopar is right," I said. "That piece of paper with the word *Henderbell* belongs to a map drawn by one of your ancestors."

"Amazing," Ava whispered, eyes on the thrones atop the stone platform.

"What is?" Enzo barked, wrinkles carved on his forehead.

"Princess Ava." She puffed her chest, staring into the distance. "I like the sound of that."

"That's what you're thinking right now?" Enzo scoffed.

"And the drawing you have," Doopar continued. "That drawing was given to me years ago by someone who is no longer a part of my life. I'm not sure why it appeared to you."

He wagged his head. "You know what." He placed the drawing in her hand. "Keep it. Just keep it. I don't have any other need for it. It showed me the way here and that's good enough for me. Think of the Santa and dragon sketch as a bonus gift."

"How do you know it'll never be of use to you again?" Doopar gazed at the drawing with longing eyes.

"I don't, but it's clear it means something to you, so keep it." Enzo fidgeted, his eyes now on me. "Do you want the piece of the map back?"

"You found it," I replied. "Keep it."

He slipped it back into his pocket and then buried his face between his hands. "Why were they taken?"

"Their absence during this time could destroy two realms," Doopar revealed.

"Destroy two realms…" Enzo mumbled and sniggered. "This has to be a joke. And I'm supposed to know what that means?"

"Do you think we're playing here, Enzo?" There was an edge to Doopar's voice. "I didn't bring you this way because I felt like having fun with strangers. If the king and queen are not sitting on their thrones on Christmas day, Henderbell and the human world of Albernaith could be exposed and destroyed by dark forces."

"But why?" Enzo asked. "Why do they carry such a burden? How can the fate of two worlds rest on the shoulders of two people sitting on those chairs?" His finger stabbed at the thrones. "They're just Grandpa and Grandma."

"No," I said. "They're the rulers of Henderbell. That's how it's always been. And on Christmas day, Henderbell and Albernaith are aligned in time, co-existing together for twenty-four hours and the Saints of Christmas must be on their thrones when that happens to bless their people."

"Saints of Christmas." He scratched the back of his head. "As in Saint Nicholas, as in Santa Claus, and my grandmother is Mrs. Claus?"

"They really dislike those names," Doopar said.

"We've been looking for them for three days," I revealed. "We've had elves camped everywhere."

"Days?" Ava was startled. "We saw them a few hours ago. We were at their house in Dorthcester."

"She's right," Enzo added, lips puckered. "It hasn't been three days yet."

"Henderbell is in another dimension of time," Doopar explained.

"Then how can both worlds align if they exist in different times?" Enzo asked.

"Think of time as a snaking river," I replied. "Each arm flowing at a different speed, but no matter the speed in which they flow, they all flow to the sea."

"I can't believe this." Enzo paced around, hands on his waist. "So are our parents..."

"They're your real parents, but they were born here," Doopar said. "Both abandoned Henderbell years ago."

"Judging your word usage, I'd have to assume they didn't leave on good terms?" Enzo nibbled on the corner of his lips.

Doopar and I exchanged a worried glance.

"So you crossed over to Henderbell by yourselves?" I asked, hoping to diverge from the subject.

"Considering the fact our grandparents were missing, yeah," Enzo replied.

"How were you able to find this exact moment in time?" I asked, the ticking of the pendulum an echo in my ear.

"I'm not sure what you mean." Enzo scowled.

"You need to know how to navigate time in order to find a desired moment to visit. It's like a sailing ship. It needs to know the sea in order to find its destination," I said. "The ability to hone such skill has been kept a secret by your family."

"We just walked inside a tree and showed up here," Ava said, tucking her hands inside the pockets of her pink coat. "I didn't even know elves existed until I saw Doopar."

"You're both telling me you just walked inside the Tree of Hender and showed up here?" I struggled to believe them.

"I swear," Enzo said. "That's what happened."

"It could be pure coincidence," Doopar mentioned.

I chose to believe them, though I wondered why their grandparents never spoke of Henderbell.

"What's that for?" Ava pointed at the pendulum.

"It tells us when Christmas arrives for Henderbell and Albernaith," I replied.

"How?" Ava asked.

"It sways all year long and only stops when both worlds are connected," I replied. "Which happens to be on Christmas day."

"I like the pin on your chest," Ava said. "I have something that looks just like it." She revealed an ornament out of her pocket.

"The sigil of Henderbell." My gaze lifted to Doopar. "This looks like Barthemeus' work?"

"Know anyone else that can make ornaments like that?" She reclined against one of the columns, arms crossed.

"Be sure to keep this one close, Ava," I said. "It's rather special."

She giggled. "You speak funny."

"I do?" I was surprised at her remark. "How so?"

"You sound like a poem," she said. "It's nice."

"Now that's the most amazing thing someone has ever said about me," I said.

The torches scattered across the room lit themselves, startling Enzo and Ava. Their reaction earned a snigger from Doopar.

"What's happening?" Ava's eyes danced in their sockets as if searching for a ghoul.

"They do that after sunset," I revealed. "Don't worry. We have no ghosts in the castle."

"So that's where they sit when they're here?" Enzo cocked his head to the thrones, cracking his fingers.

"Yes," I answered. "They're made of crystal, forged by King Oden after he conquered Henderbell." The flames burning on the candelabras beside the thrones casted dancing shadows on their surfaces.

"And the antlers rising behind them?" Enzo asked.

"A tribute to Kurah, the elk," I replied.

"The big marble statue wasn't enough?" he asked, raising his shoulders.

"And what are these drawings on the stone platform?" Ava asked. "They look like people with their hands raised."

"King Oden had them carved as a reminder that Henderbell was to always be the most powerful country, crushing anyone who opposed its ideals," I replied.

"Was he a tyrant?" Enzo frowned.

My head jerked back at his question. "No, he was a good king."

Ava observed the thrones with great fascination.

"Do you want to go up there?" I asked.

"Can I?" Her voice beamed with excitement.

"Of course…"

She ran up the platform before I even finished answering, her footsteps echoing around the room. She jumped over the last step, landing between both thrones. Her feet remained rooted to their spot for a while as she gazed at the sight. She approached the throne on the left, her hands running across its arm then touching the antler rising from the back. "This looks way better than the couch in their living room, Enzo!" Her words boomed.

"Couldn't agree more!" Enzo shouted.

She sat on the throne, legs dangling above the ground. With a puffed chest, she smiled, her eyes scanning the entire room. A chill shot down my body. She couldn't hide what was going on in her mind. She enjoyed the view from up there.

I watched them as if gazing at a living dream. Fascination always consumed me when I heard tales of the Griffins in Albernaith. I was one of the few who knew of their existence. I had never met someone born in that world. And yet, here before me stood Prince Enzo and Princess Ava.

"Doopar, would you mind going to Loomstak?" I asked. "He needs to know they're here."

"Are they still on the other side of the forest?" she asked, fixing the belt around her waist.

"No." I hesitated and said, "The Prison of Krishmar."

She scowled at my response. "We already looked near the prison. Why would you send him and his men there again? They can't even go inside—"

"Just...please," I insisted. "I need him to know the grandchildren are here."

"Of course," Doopar replied, looking at me as if aware my answer lacked honesty. "I'll go meet them at once."

"Do come back as soon as you find them," I said.

"Shouldn't I stay with the rest of them?" Doopar asked.

"No, no!" Ava shouted from the platform, still sitting on the throne. "Please come back."

"I think you're needed here," I said with a smirk.

"I'll be back soon, Ava." Doopar said. "I promise."

"She won't take long. Elves are the speediest beings in Henderbell," I mentioned, Doopar's lips turning into a smug smile.

"Be careful." Enzo scratched the back of his head. "It's...well, it could be...dangerous, I guess." He tilted his head to the side. "I'll be waiting here."

"Thank you." Doopar seemed surprised at his concern. "By the way, Ishmael knew your father well. Maybe you should ask him a few questions." I wished Doopar had refrained her words. "I'll see you all soon."

She gave me a smirk and walked toward the door.

"So you knew my father?" Enzo asked the moment Doopar was out of the room.

"I did," I replied, watching Ava jump from the throne and walk down the stone platform.

"And my mother?" he insisted.

"Not as well as Bane. My time with your mother was short, but I lived ten years with your father. He was twenty-two when he left."

"I guess you didn't leave things on good terms?" he asked with a shrug, hands tucked in his pockets.

"It's a long story and I don't want to bash your own father," I said, Ava now standing beside her brother, face burning with curiosity.

"I don't think you could damage his image more than he already has." His words carried sorrow.

"I think it's time you learned more about your family," I said.

"Can you tell us more?" Ava asked.

"I can show you."

# ENZO

# CHAPTER 11

My curiosity spiked as Ava and I followed Ishmael to a door on the far right of the thrones. Carved on its surface was a king and a queen. In their hands sat staffs with antlers rising from their tips. How could I have lived all these years without a single suspicion of my family's truth?

"Behind these doors is the Hall of Rulers. Only those of royal blood can enter this place." Ishmael twisted the golden knob. "I was only allowed to venture beyond this point after your grandparents took me in."

My pulse thudded in my ear, heart pounding fast. In front of me was a long hallway with six columns on each side. They supported a roof covered with a colorful mural depicting a winter forest during sunset. At their feet were bowls of iron filled with burning coal. Tall wooden doors were scattered on each side, and in between them were framed paintings. At the end of the hall was an enormous stained glass window depicting an elk standing amidst a green forest.

"Welcome to your side of the castle." He beckoned the way with a wave, his words triggering a smile on my face.

"My side?" Ava looked left and right while walking through the doorway. I followed her, my every step feeling like a dream.

"Anyone of royal blood living in Henderbell calls this place home," Ishmael explained as he shut the door behind us. "No commoners are allowed in here."

"So this is where Dad lived?" Ava's eyes scanned the roof.

"You're correct." Ishmael pointed at one of the doors. "That used to be his room. Mine was the one next to it. Circumstances forced me to move to the other side of the castle."

"This place is beautiful," Ava mumbled. "Mr. Wombington would love it here."

Her last words disrupted my amazement.

"Who's Mr. Wombington?" Ishmael asked.

"Her teddy bear." I rolled my eyes. "They took it when they kidnapped our grandparents."

"He's my friend." Ava pursed her lips, a downcast look on her face. "I hope he's alright."

"We'll find him," Ishmael said.

How could Ava think of that tattered teddy bear when we were in here?

Every frame on the wall was different. A few were white, their surfaces smooth, while others were gold with carved patterns and swirls. The portraits painted on the canvases were so detailed, they could pass for photographs.

"I assume the people in the paintings are my family?" I asked, hoping my assumption was correct.

"Yes, they are," he replied. "Your ancestors were born in Lestee, the country east of Henderbell. The Griffins were the first Lesteenians to cross the Crystal Sea and settle on this side of the world."

He led us to a painting depicting a man with a long white beard, eyes as golden as a fall leaf. He was dressed in a scarlet robe, a gold pin shaped like an elk's head on his chest.

"This is King Oden, the first Griffin to step foot in this country five hundred years ago."

"The guy who defeated Claudius the Fallen," I added.

My words earned a scowl. He gazed at me, apparently surprised.

"Doopar told me about him," I said with a shrug, proud of being able to remember that piece of information.

"You're a good listener," he continued. "King Oden crossed the Crystal Sea claiming he had seen this side of the world in a dream. The story goes on to say Kurah the elk, appeared to him in a dream and chose him to rule the world beyond uncharted waters. Many thought he was insane since he already ruled Moonrar. But to him, he had seen more than a dream. He had heard Kurah's voice. He gathered his armies and crossed the Crystal Sea only to discover Henderbell was already populated and ruled by a tyrant, Claudius the Fallen. He managed to remain hidden for quite some time, since Henderbell never received visitors from Lestee before. In secret, Oden and his army plotted an attack that defeated Claudius in what Henderbellian history calls the War of Swords. Your family has been sitting on this throne ever since." He walked past a few paintings, Ava and I at his heels. "And here we have your grandfather, King Nicholas."

"He looks so different." Ava touched the golden canvas. "So young."

The painting depicted Grandpa dressed in a purple robe, his wavy raven hair falling down his shoulders, the Henderbellian sigil pinned to his chest, lips pulled into a mysterious grin.

"I don't think I've ever seen him with hair like that before." I mentioned.

"I like the jewels on his beard," Ava added. "They look like ornaments on a Christmas tree."

"Of course you'd like those," I remarked.

"He should wear clothes like these more often," Ava continued.

"Is my father's portrait also here?" I scanned the room, the thought of seeing his face felt like a brick crushing my head.

"Yes," Ishmael replied in a low voice.

"And my mother?" I asked.

"No. Her portrait can't be displayed here."

"Why not?" Ava asked, hands on her waist.

"They didn't marry in Henderbell," he replied, gaze on Grandpa's portrait. "She isn't considered a part of the royal family." His chest lifted with a breath. "They left a lot of responsibilities behind when they abandoned this place."

"But why did they leave?" Ava asked.

"Princess, I don't think I should—"

"Please answer." A flush of adrenaline spread down my body. "We may be young but we aren't stupid."

"Your father no longer wanted to rule after he met your mother," he started after a brief silence. "And neither did she. They renounced their claim to the throne and fled to Albernaith. There was no warning from them. One day they were here and the next they weren't."

"I'm sure there's more to that story," I retorted.

"That's what I was told," he said. "In the ten years your father and I lived together in this castle, all he ever talked about was how much he looked forward to being king one day."

"How did you end up living here?" My question made him lose his composure. His eyes scanned the walls and the portraits, finally landing on me again.

"Your grandparents took me in after my parents died fighting the Shadow Spirits."

"I'm sorry," I said, my gaze shying away from him.

"It was a long time ago," he said, the ghosts of his past haunting his eyes.

"Is Grandma here?" Ava asked.

"She's on the other wall, where all the queens are. Did you..."

Ishmael's words were drowned by the sight of a familiar face on one of the portraits: my father's. Even from a few feet away, I distinguished his face, despite the unusual look of joy stamped on it. The burning flames inside the iron bowls at the foot of the pillar casted shadows over his canvas.

Ishmael and Ava chattered as they walked to the opposite side, their words turning to muffled sounds as I neared my father's painting.

The brown eyes were still the same, the joy displayed in them a forgotten memory. The smile on his lips looked like a forgotten dream. His hair was tied into a bun, with a braid on the side.

"When did he ever wear bright colors?" I whispered, observing the yellow swirls scattered on his dark blue garments.

I wished I had known the man in front me. My memories were of an absent father, always working, mind set on everything else but his family. His rage-filled screams were what I'd remember most for the rest of my life.

Blood boiled in my veins.

"I hope you do disappear." My hands clenched into fists. "Even if we somehow save this place, I hope I never have to see you again."

"Enzo!" Ava's booming voice stole my attention. "Come see Grandma's picture!"

I glanced into my father's eyes one more time before going to them.

"Are you alright?" Ishmael asked.

"Yes, just happened to see a face I wasn't planning on seeing," I replied. "Anyway, so this was my grandmother?" I tucked my hands in my pockets, grasping the parchment paper.

"Yes," Ishmael answered.

"Of course she'd be wearing that." I nodded, disapproving of the platinum cone-shaped hairdo. Her pink garments did a great job at accentuating her gold necklace.

"Isn't her yellow lipstick beautiful?" Ava mentioned. "I want one."

"Sure," I said with a smirk, hoping my face didn't reflect the rage of emotions stirring inside me. "Beautiful…"

"Don't let hate build a house in your heart," Ishmael said, making it extremely clear my rage was on full display. "I know your father isn't perfect but—"

"Didn't he leave you, too?" I waved my hand in dismissal of his comment. "Why do you defend him?"

I couldn't understand why he was so inclined to defend the man who abandoned him.

"What good does bitterness do?" he asked.

"None, but being stupid doesn't help either." My cheeks flushed. "Are we done? We just met. I think it's a little too early for you to give me advice."

"I advise your grandparents. That's my job."

"I guess you're on vacation then, because I don't see them anywhere," I snapped.

He stared, quiet, mouth parted. His nod of disapproval triggered my anger. Who did he think he was?

"Ava, how about we take a look at your father's portrait? I think Enzo needs to be alone for a while."

"Okay," she mumbled, walking alongside Ishmael.

"Can we go see something else?" I requested, fingers laced behind my head.

"After the princess is done," Ishmael replied.

"Great." I rolled my eyes.

I strolled down the hall, observing the other portraits, but amidst all the colorful art was a black canvas. Carved on its frame were trees, their crooked branches forming suffering human faces: some cried, others screamed, a few seemed to be in anguish. Why was such a sinister sight displayed with my family? The canvas held my attention until Ishmael and my sister walked to stand beside me.

"What's this?" I asked him, haunted by the carved faces.

"It looks scary," Ava added.

"Now that's a secret only your grandparents can share," Ishmael said.

"Why?" I insisted.

"It's a family secret. Though I live in the castle, I'm not blood." Disappointment shrouded his face. "I wish I could tell you, but it's not my place."

I scanned the strange sight one more time, each somber detail somehow a reminder of the lingering doom revealed to me.

"Can you take us to a very high tower so we can see the whole city?" Ava requested.

"It's pretty dark outside," Ishmael replied. "I don't think we'd be able to see much, but dinner should be ready soon."

He snapped his fingers twice. I was startled by two flames rising from one of the iron bowls at the foot of a column. They twirled in the air, spreading out to form two human shapes. Fire turned to golden armor and flesh. Their faces were as pale as a blank page, eyes the color of the sunset. One of them was a bald man, chin chiseled, shoulders broad. The woman's golden locks were like a sunflower, her lips the color of blood.

"How may we be of service?" asked the knight in a deep voice, his face rigid.

"Mandeerun, Ashtolia, allow me to—"

"I couldn't help but overhear you talking, Ishmael," said the knight. "Welcome, Prince Enzo and Princess Ava. We've heard so much about you."

"So you actually know who we are," I said, afraid their eyes could actually slice me open.

"We're one of the few who do," Ashtolia added.

"You're so beautiful." Ava observed her reflection on his armor.

"Thank you, princess," Mandeerun said. "If I were human and my face not made of fire, you'd probably see me blushing."

Ava snickered.

"We're honored to finally have you here in the castle," Ashtolia said, grasping the handle of the sword on her waist.

"Do we still have clothes that fit them somewhere?" Ishmael asked. "Both are in need of a change."

"We should have a few choices for the prince in Bane's old bedroom," Mandeerun replied. "They should be inside the wardrobe."

"I believe we may have a few things for the princess inside Queen Mary's old wardrobe as well," Ashtolia said.

"Perfect." Ishmael clapped his hands, the reflection of the burning flames causing the Henderbellian sigil on his chest to glimmer. "Go get dressed and meet me in the throne room."

"We'll stand guard as you both change," Mandeerun said as Ishmael walked away. "We'll wait for you here in the hall."

"So where's my dad's old room again?" I asked, wondering what else I'd find in there besides old clothes.

"To the right of the Bending Shield." Mandeerun pointed at the black canvas responsible for spiking my curiosity.

"And you'll be going in there, princess." Ashtolia pointed to the door on the opposite side.

The strange canvas held my attention as I twisted the knob on the door and entered the room.

The large geometric window provided a view of the starlit sky. Blue silk curtains draped beside it, spilling on the floor. At the foot of the window was a beige couch. The bed frame was made of chestnut wood, carved in the shape of two antlers. The nightstand beside it was of the same color, its legs shaped like winged dragons. Constellations were painted across the ceiling, a crystal candle-lit chandelier at the center. The walls were covered in scarlet swirls, spreading all across the room.

To my right was a bookshelf placed beside an old dresser. Next to one of the books was a necklace with a locket shaped like an eight-pointed star.

I picked up the curious object, holding it at eye level. It was silver, its surface carved with thin lines resembling the roots of a tree. I put it back and opened the wardrobe where I found my father's old clothes.

After looking through the drawers, I picked a blue collared long sleeve shirt, black pants, and a pair of boots. There was also a tattered gray coat that fit perfectly, the sigil of Henderbell sown on its back.

I folded the clothes I was wearing before, put them inside the wardrobe and stepped out of the room only to be startled by Ava standing inches away from me.

"I was about to knock on that door!" she squealed.

"You look—wow!" I suppressed a laugh. Of course she picked the most eccentric outfit I'd ever seen: a bright pink coat, a suede yellow long sleeve, blue pants, and red boots.

"Be honest." She twirled. "Don't I look like a real princess."

"You sure do." I tapped her on the shoulder. "Alright, time for dinner."

"We'll be here when you come back," Mandeerun said, still as a statue, Ashtolia beside him.

My eyes scanned the portraits on the wall as we walked down the hall, amazed and frightened of my family's history. Once inside the throne room, I spotted Ishmael at the foot of the stone platform, staring at the thrones as if in distant thought.

He smiled and said, "Those look much better on you."

"Do you like my coat?" Ava twirled. "Is it royal enough?"

Ishmael chuckled and said, "You remind me a lot of your grandmother. Always cheerful."

"And always wearing something extremely bright," I added.

"I hope you're both hungry," he said. "They're preparing—"

The doors bust open. Voices boomed as two guards appeared, holding a body covered in torn clothing and dirt, the draping silver hair covering the face. My knees trembled once I realized it was Doopar. They held her by the arms, her feet dragging on the floor, head down. The belt that held her sword wasn't with her.

"What in Kurah's name happened?" Ishmael rushed her way.

Ava stared with a parted mouth, face pale.

"We found her in the forest," revealed one of the guards. "She's somewhat conscious but she can't speak."

"Is she going to die, Enzo?" Ava tugged at my sleeve. "Look at her!"

"I am," I shuddered as feeling slowly escaped my body.

"Doopar." Ishmael held her face between the palms of his hands. "What happened? Can you hear me?"

She groaned and squirmed, her purple eyes bulging out of their sockets, the veins on her neck visible beneath her skin.

Fear gripped me as blood spewed out of her mouth, forming a scarlet puddle by her feet. I had drawn characters dying, written death scenes, but witnessing such a gruesome sight made me realize death could go from a simple thought to a close threat in seconds.

Ishmael grabbed me by the shoulder. "Stay here with your sister. I have to take Doopar to Mandeerun and Ashtolia."

I nodded, my limbs shaking.

"You're safe." He looked at Ava. "You're both safe."

"Don't let her die." Ava's eyes glistened. "Please."

Ishmael took a hard look at her, a frown carved on his forehead. "I'll try my best."

He grabbed Doopar's arm and laid it over his shoulder. "I've got her. Go back to your posts!"

"At once," said one of the soldiers, his cheek and armor stained with blood.

Both soldiers walked out of the room when Ishmael was out of sight.

Ava fiddled her fingers, gazing at the expanding puddle of blood on the floor.

"What do you think happened to her?" she whispered with a wobbling chin.

"I—I don't—" I swallowed my words. "I don't know..."

The ticking of the pendulum echoed louder in the hovering silence between us. The scarlet puddle was a magnet for Ava's attention. And my heart was ensnared by confusion and fear.

"Ava." My voice echoed.

"What?" she mumbled, face pale.

"Let's sit here." I guided her to the platform, sitting on the first few steps at the bottom.

"Okay," she mumbled.

I placed an arm around her shoulder, holding her head against my chest so she wouldn't stare at the gruesome sight. I searched for a thought that could assure me everything was going to be alright, but the moving pendulum became a constant reminder of our approaching doom.

The door leading to the Hall of Rulers opened. Ishmael emerged, the red blood stains on his purple garments stealing my breath for a few seconds.

Ava whimpered as he approached with a frown.

"Mandeerun and Ashtolia are looking after her." He cleared his throat with a nod of disappointment. "But she won't speak. No one knows what happened to her."

"Will she survive?" Ava sniffled.

Ishmael's gaze turned to the blood. He took in a long breath and said, "I don't know."

"Did you hear anything about the elves she was supposed to meet?" Ava asked.

"No." His face grew rigid. "I haven't."

"You think they're dead?" she continued.

"I hope not." He pressed his eyes shut and wagged his head. "Someone very dear to me was with them. The thought that he may have died…"

"What do we do now?" I shot up to my feet. "We can't just sit here and wait," I contested. "You said Christmas will arrive in six days, right?"

"Five after midnight," he mentioned.

"Can't we send out an army or something?" I asked.

"I'm not dispatching an army before I know what happened," Ishmael replied. "That's suicide."

My hands clenched into fists.

"Go to your rooms," he continued. "I'll bring you some food. Don't leave them until I come find you."

# CHAPTER 12

Muffled groans and gurgles came from behind one of the doors as Ava and I rushed down the Hall of Rulers. We halted at the eerie sounds, my mind scurrying to find any thought or idea that could defeat my fear. But there was nothing.

I leaned closer, my ear a hair away from touching the door. Though I couldn't hear much, I was able to pick up a few words.

"Hold her down!" Mandeerun shouted.

"I'm trying!" Ashtolia retorted.

"We need to find a way for her to speak…"

I stepped away, wishing I could discover a way to peer inside Doopar's head to see what happened.

Ava's face was as pale as a dove's feather. She fiddled with her fingers, nibbling on the corner of her lips.

"Hey." I touched her shoulder, leading her away from the door. "I'm sure we'll have more news about Doopar soon."

She forced a smile.

We approached my father's old bedroom. I glanced at the Bending Shield before entering, my eyes quickly surveying the suffering faces on the frame's engraved edges, the canvas dark and somber.

Ava's eyes scanned the constellations painted on the ceiling as soon as we were inside. I sat on the edge of the bed, heart still pounding.

"Can you believe this room used to belong to him?" I asked, hoping to sway her mind away from all the gore she had seen.

"Not really." She approached the bookshelf, grabbing a book. "He's the least magical person I've ever met."

My attention turned to the geometric window, my eyes following the collection of stars spread across the night sky.

"What's this?"

I followed Ava's voice. She held the necklace with the pendant shaped like an eight-pointed star.

"Not sure," I replied. "I found it on the bookshelf."

She sat beside me, object in hand. "It's pretty." She held it at eye level. "I like the details on it. Think it belonged to Dad?"

A knock sounded on the door.

Ishmael walked in, bringing with him the smell of cooked meat. He wheeled in a silver tray on a table, each of its legs carved in the shape of men dressed in robes.

"I hope you like endybird." He stopped the tray in front of me and uncovered the food. I noticed the blood stains on his clothes were gone. The meat was set on two white plates, a fork and a knife beside each one. Though I had never heard of an endybird before, the meat looked—and smelled—like chicken.

"Whatever this is, it smells delicious." Ava set the locket on the bed.

"Sorry you have to eat in this room. I was going to have you at the dining hall, but given our current circumstances, it's best you remain hidden."

Ava struggled to cut her meat. After a few seconds, she dropped the utensils and ate with her hands, holding the meat by the bone.

Ishmael stared at something beside me. I followed his gaze, spotting the locket.

"I'm going to assume you've seen it before," I asked, mouth full.

"No," he answered sharply. "I haven't. Where was it?"

"Here in the room," I answered. "It was on that bookshelf behind you."

"It's a beautiful locket." He crossed his arms, a frown on his forehead. "The octagram is a special symbol."

"Ah, so that's what the shape is called," I said, taking another bite of endybird.

Ishmael stood to his feet. "Well, I'll leave you two to finish your dinner. We'll speak in the morning. I'll have Ashtolia and Mandeerun keep guard outside."

The octagram held my attention as I ate. Something drew me to the object. Staring at it was like looking at the face of an old friend. If every single one of its eight points had a secret, I was willing to listen.

I walked Ava to her bedroom after we finished the food. Mandeerun and Ashtolia stood in the hall like statues.

"You're going to be okay?" I asked, reclining my shoulder on the doorway, arms folded over my chest. "You could take the bed. I could sleep on that couch by the window."

"I'll be fine." She rolled her eyes. "I'll knock if I need anything."

"Alright. Goodnight."

"Night."

I returned to my room, freshened up, and found some sleeping clothes inside the wardrobe—my mind still haunted by questions surrounding Doopar.

The necklace with the octagram-shaped pendant fell on the floor as I got under the covers. I picked up the object and held it close to my face. After fiddling it between my fingers for a while, I placed it inside one of the drawers on the nightstand.

I tossed and turned, waiting for sleep to find me, but the memory of the emptiness in her eyes didn't allow me to close mine. Though my body was tired, my mind was troubled and ready to run a race.

I gave up on sleeping and walked to the bookshelf. The titles on the spines of the books were visible, despite the dim light of the candles burning on the crystal chandelier. There were books on ancient Henderbellian history, poems, and symbology. I was about to retrieve one when a knock startled me.

I looked through the peephole, Ava and Ashtolia on the other side.

"Hey, are you alright?" I asked after opening the door.

Ava nibbled on her bottom lip, hands crossed behind her back. She rocked her body back and forth, standing on the tip of her toes. Her pajamas were neon yellow with orange flowers stitched to the silky fabric.

She nudged Ashtolia on the hip after a brief silence and said, "Can you ask him?"

Ashtolia frowned, Ava's reflection displayed on her golden armor.

"The princess would like to know if she could sleep in your room tonight." Her posture was like that of a war general, chest puffed, head high.

"Sure," I said, brows arched. "But since you're speaking on behalf of my sister, can you ask her why she needed you to ask?"

"She overheard a conversation I was having with Mandeerun and discovered what a royal decree is," she replied with a deadpan face. "So she asked if I could make a royal decree and have her sleep in your room...tonight."

"Please, Enzo." Ava grabbed my arm. "Mr. Wombington is missing and I hate sleeping alone. Please?"

"I thought I offered before," I reminded her. "And you said you were going to be okay by yourself."

"Yes, but I declined your offer and now I want the offer again. I realized I didn't want to be by myself here."

"Is this decree official?" I reclined on the doorframe.

"I'm afraid so," Astholia answered.

"Then sure, come on—"

"Thank you, thank you!" Ava darted into the room.

"I guess I'll sleep on that couch by the window after all." I scratched the back of my head.

"I'll be out here if you need me," Ashtolia said. "Good night."

I closed the door. Ava was already under the covers, only half of her face in view.

"Well, good night," I said.

"Night!"

I laid down on the couch and gazed at the star-lit sky, now covered in streaks of purple and yellow, the sight a resemblance of an aurora borealis. Whenever silence settled, it was pierced by the sound of Ava tossing around on the bed. But the stillness of the night and my attempt to fall asleep disappeared after a predatory roar.

Ava jumped up, kneeling on the bed. "Did you hear that?" she asked with a shiver.

The hair-raising sound bellowed one more time before I could answer. Footsteps followed on the other side of the door, accompanied by the sound of rattling chains. A moving shadow appeared between the gap of the door and the floor.

Ava's breaths grew heavier. She grabbed the covers and clutched them as if they could save her.

I tiptoed my way to the door and looked through the peephole. My feet fumbled back at the nightmare lingering on the other side: Burning embers clung to its human-like skeletal body, and in its hands, a chain dropping down to its feet. Horns of many sizes rose from its head. Its eyes were round and white.

"What did you see?" Ava asked, half of her face hidden behind the covers.

Silence.

"Enzo?" she insisted with a whimper.

"Shh." I held up a finger. "Quiet."

The shadows displayed between the bottom gap of the door stopped moving. The door clattered as the creature pounded repeatedly.

I rushed toward her, grabbed her wrist and crawled under the bed, my teeth bearing into my lips. Ava's chin trembled, her breaths heavy and short.

It was as if my heart was going to explode with every blow on the door. Where were Mandeerun and Ashtolia? Ishmael? Anyone?

Gurgles and moans replaced the pounding. Scratches followed. The doorknob rattled. Ava squeezed my hand at the creaking sound of the hinges.

A pungent smell crawled into my nostrils once the macabre being entered the room, its toenails brown and curved downward, skin covered in thin orange streaks glowing like lava. I gritted my teeth as the creature paced impatiently.

A sharp screech stole a shudder from me. The creature moved toward the window, leaving the open door unguarded.

I glanced at Ava and cocked my head toward the door. She squeezed my hand even tighter and nodded in disagreement. She suppressed a scream when the beast jumped on the bed, its growl accompanied by the sound of cracking wood.

If I didn't find a way to get this creature out of the room, we were both going to die. But better one alive than both dead.

"Stay here," I mouthed, jerking my hand away from her grasp. "Don't move."

She tried grabbing my wrist, but I pulled away.

I took in a breath, crawled from under the bed, and darted out of the room.

I didn't dare look back.

A loud roar pierced my ears.

Rhythmic thuds were followed by the rattling of chains.

It was coming after me.

I glanced over my shoulder. Its wide white eyes seemed to have the power to take my life with a simple glance. The creature spread out its long arms and leapt on the wall, one hand clawing at the surface, the other holding a chain. It rushed after me like a crawling lizard.

A sinking feeling wrapped my stomach as its roars invaded my ears. I ran as fast as I could, eyes on the door leading into the throne room.

Frames clashed on the ground as the creature pursued me. I chanced a look back. It leapt from the wall back to the floor, thrusting the chain out of its grip. Metal turned to flesh, taking the shape of a long body. It had a sharp snout, scarlet eyes, and a two-forked tongue.

My pace quickened, but the slithering nightmare was faster.

This was it.

This was going to be my end.

An explosion stole feeling from my limbs, setting off a ringing in my ears. Countless scarlet threads hovered behind me, one by one fading into thin air. The snake and its owner were nowhere to be seen. Doopar was on the opposite side of the destruction, a dagger in hand, my sister running in my direction. Ava threw her arms around me before I could say a word to Doopar.

"Are you alright?" I asked, scanning her face for any bruises or wounds while my heart pounded against my ribcage.

"Yes, yes," she replied behind shallow breaths. "When I saw Doopar walking down the hall from under the bed, I crawled out and stood by the doorway." Her attention shifted to Doopar, her purple coat still smeared with blood. "She stabbed that creature on her back." She smiled. "She saved us."

The flames from the iron bowls reflected in Doopar's glistening eyes. "I'm sorry." She knelt down and tucked the dagger inside her mud-stained boot.

"For?" I asked.

"For bringing that abomination into the castle." Her gaze remained on the ground. "I'm sorry I put you both in danger. I tried to regain control of my body but I couldn't." Her hands trembled as they curled into fists. "That abomination entered this castle through me. What you saw was a Soul Drainer, servants of the Shadow Spirits. They've been extinct for hundreds of years. They despise elves and can use my kind as a host. It entered my body and robbed me of my ability to speak, though I could still see everything." She let out a shudder. "I wanted to scream as the guards dragged me into the castle, but I couldn't."

"How did it find you?" I asked, relieved to see her back to her former self.

"I was on my way to find Loomstak as Ishmael commanded," she replied. "My body shifted to snow once I was out of the gates. All I remember was a dark cloud robbing me of my movements. And then I was here in the throne room. I could see everything, but I had no control over my body."

"Did you ever reach Loomstak?" I asked.

"No," she answered. "I believe—"

The door busted open. Ishmael emerged, his right cheek covered in blood, his hair bun undone, wisps falling over his face. He ran to Doopar, throwing his arms around her.

"You're alive," he whispered.

She gave him a trembling smile.

"We have to leave," he said, despair stamped on his face. "Go grab some clothes. It's cold. We have to leave now."

"What happened to you?" I asked, my pulse pounding in my ear.

"Two Soul Drainers were in the castle," he replied behind heavy breaths. "You can't stay here."

"One just attacked them." Doopar's face went rigid.

"So there are more?" he asked.

"I'm not sure," Doopar replied.

"How did you recover so fast?" Ishmael frowned.

"The Soul Drainer used me as a host to get inside the castle," she revealed, each word carrying disappointment and shame.

"No, no, no." Ishmael pressed the heels of his hands to his forehead. "Where are Mandeerun and Ashtolia?"

"Probably dead," Doopar said.

"Did you find Loomstak?"

"I didn't have enough time to reach him," she answered.

Ishmael's posture stooped forward, mouth parted. "Go change! *Go!*" he insisted. "We have to leave now. I'll be in front of the Bending Shield."

We rushed back to our rooms, put on the clothes we had worn earlier, and met Doopar and Ishmael in front of the eerie canvas beside my dad's old bedroom.

"How are we leaving the castle unseen?" Doopar asked.

Ishmael swiped his hand before the Bending Shield, triggering the tortured faces carved on the golden frame to move as though life found them. Ripples spread across the darkness of the canvas as the frame expanded until a few inches taller than Ishmael.

"This is our way out of the castle," Ishmael said. "King Nicholas created it. No one else in this castle knows about it. It was made in case the royal family needed to escape. Now come on."

Ishmael disappeared behind the darkness. More ripples scattered across the surface once he was out of sight. Doopar followed, Ava and I at her heels.

# CHAPTER 13

The cold air wrapped me like a blanket. Snow crunched beneath my feet as I stepped into a pine tree forest illuminated by the moonlit sky. I glanced over my shoulder, thinking the canvas would still be there, but only the wintry landscape was in view.

"Where are we?" Ava asked, her breath steaming out of her mouth.

"The Forest of Nick," Ishmael answered.

"Why here?" Doopar asked.

Ishmael knelt on the ground and at the sway of his hand, a beam of light appeared, breaking the darkness, tracing the shape of an elk's head. The earth marked by the symbol thinned like the mist, revealing a downward staircase made of stone.

"Come with me." He walked down the steps.

We followed, entering an underground hideaway. There were shelves packed with bread and jars full of water. Under them were cabinets with many drawers. Eight mounted sets of armor were lined up against the wall to my right, its surface covered in swords, spears, bows, and arrows. Beside them was a bookshelf. There were beds to my left with trunks at their feet. A table with eight chairs sat in the middle. Candles burned on the scattered candelabras.

"What is this place?" Ava asked with a dazed look, removing her pink coat and hanging it on the coat rack. We all followed her act.

"A shelter for the King's family. King Nicholas and Queen Mary built it after the Shadow Spirits attacked twenty-five years ago. In here are also a few of the most prized possessions of the Griffin family," Ishmael revealed. "All of these weapons, armors, and books belong to your ancestors."

"Why didn't you bring us here before?" I asked, my footsteps creaking on the wooden floor. "Seems a lot safer than the castle."

"Our enemies already had what they wanted. There was no reason for them to return to the castle." He walked to the table, pulled a chair and took a seat, elbows on his knees, head bowed.

"Unless they know about Enzo and Ava," Doopar added.

Her comment sent a chill down my body.

Ishmael's hand slid down his face. "Let's hope that's not true."

Doopar let out a pain-filled groan, followed by a wince.

"How are you feeling?" I asked.

"Every muscle hurts," she replied, not daring to look me in the eye. "My mouth tastes like blood, but I'm sure I'll survive."

She was about to walk to the table when I grabbed her wrist, our eyes locking. "It wasn't your fault."

My words earned a frown. "Part of it was," she retorted. "I should've been more cautious. I should've seen the signs of their return. I fought my whole life to be a warrior and now that I am, I failed at one of the most important tasks of my life."

"But had it not been for you, my sister and I would've probably been lost in that forest." I smiled. "Maybe we would've both been dead."

She pulled her hand away. "That's no excuse. I should've been more careful."

"Enzo's right, Doopar. There were no signs pointing to the resurrection of the Soul Drainers," Ishmael revealed, eyes distant. "I spent the last few days pouring over those books and maps in the Room of Secrets. I read those notes they left on the thrones over and over. Nothing. Absolutely nothing. Had I known, I wouldn't have sent—" His words were interrupted by a ragged breath. "Well, I would've done things differently."

"Don't speak as if they're dead." Doopar sat beside him. "We don't know—"

"That's the problem," Ishmael barked. "We don't know anything, but we can assume if they aren't dead, they're being used by the Shadow Spirits, Soul Drainers, and whatever other devilries are with them." He shook his head. "He was reluctant about going. And I ordered him to go anyway. Even if Henderbellian law forbade it."

"Who was?" Ava asked, walking closer to him.

"Loomstak," Ishmael wagged his head in disappointment. "The general of the elven army...the elf I love. I sent the one who has my heart to his doom..."

Ava grabbed his hand.

"You promised me you were going to help me find Mr. Wombington," she whispered with a determined stare. "And I promise you, we'll help you find Loomstak."

"Thank you, princess." He smiled sadly, holding her hand between his own.

"You're sure we're safe in here?" I walked to the bookshelf, the flames on the candelabra beside it casting moving shadows over the books.

"Safest place we could be right now," he said. "It's hidden by magic."

"Magic," I whispered with a slight headshake. I wasn't sure if I'd ever get used to the idea of my family having magic in their blood.

"So what do we do now?" Ava asked.

"Now we need to rest," Ishmael replied. "We'll decide our next steps in the morning."

"Don't think I'll be getting much sleep tonight," Ava said as I scanned the spines of the books. "I think I'll have nightmares," she continued. "Mr. Wombington used to talk to me when I had bad dreams."

"Don't worry," Ishmael said. "We won't leave you."

"I'm starving," Doopar said. "I feel like I haven't eaten in days."

"Is the bread still good?" I asked.

"The bread is always good in here," Ishmael revealed, his right eyebrow curved into an arch.

"Let me guess." I smirked. "Magic?"

"Every morning, the leftovers are exchanged by fresh food. The jars are refilled with water and wine."

The bread was cut in slices, set on a round wooden tray. I brought it to the table and returned to the shelf to grab a few cups and a jar of water.

After we were done eating in silence, we each picked a bed for the night: I picked the one on the far right, next to the wall; Ava the one next to me, and Ishmael and Doopar the beds on the far left. The trunks were stocked with towels, soap, and fresh linens. There was a door next to one of the armors that led to some sort of bathroom. Warm water trickled from a ceiling of dark rocks. There was a toilet, a sink, and a mirror. We each freshened up before going to sleep.

Though tired, my mind still burst with energy. All I ever wanted for the last four years was to escape the reality of my house. I wanted to be free from the screams, the fights, and the smell of alcohol that lingered after my dad came home. But now I wished I could find a way to fix everything. It was one thing to wish for freedom, another to wish for a second chance.

I tossed and turned for what felt like hours, trying to get some shuteye, but my mind beat me at this wrestling game. I glanced at the coat rack, scanning the ragged gray coat that belonged to my father. What were his days like when he lived in Henderbell? What was it like to grow up as a prince?

The sight of Ava sleeping caught my attention. She had her hands wrapped around something. I leaned closer to get a better view. It was the ornament shaped like the Henderbellian sigil.

"Can't sleep?" Doopar's voice startled me. She sat on the floor beside a bookshelf facing the beds, a book on her lap and a pile beside her.

"Didn't see you there."

"I noticed." Her eyes remained on the pages.

Ishmael slept with hands crossed over his chest like a corpse in a coffin. If not for his breathing, I would've thought he was dead.

"Does he always sleep like that?" I whispered.

She glanced at Ishmael and smiled. "Ever since he was a kid." Her gaze met mine. "Are you going to stay there or are you planning on sitting next to me?"

"Not sure if you're being serious," I said.

"Would it stop you if I wasn't?"

"Only if you didn't want me." My eyes leapt from my sockets. "I mean—if you didn't want me to sit beside—"

"Just sit here, Enzo." She nodded.

My cheeks burned. I walked to her, hoping my brain would retain its ability to speak. I noticed the words *The History of the Shadow Spirits* on the header of the book on her lap as I sat beside her.

"Found anything relevant?" I asked, legs crossed, elbows on my knees.

"Nothing," she said, seemingly defeated. "I've read this a thousand times. I'm going over it again for any clues, but nothing yet. It's frustrating, really."

"How did they come to be?" I asked. "These Shadow Spirits?"

Ava rolled on the bed, letting out a long sigh. I thought she was awake for a moment, but then she started snoring.

"There are many tales on the origins of the Shadow Spirits. Unfortunately, history is written by those who win wars. So you never get the opposition's side, only the victor's tale. And it's their version that's claimed to be truth." She closed the book, setting it on top of the pile beside her. "I can share with you what I know—at least what I was taught."

"Sounds like you don't believe what you know." The candles on the candelabra cast shadows on her face.

"I just think there's a version of the story we haven't heard yet."

"Then tell me the version you know and believe."

"The Shadow Spirits came from across the Crystal Sea in human form thirty years after King Oden conquered Henderbell. They tread the sea in search of new land to expand their kingdom. Only they weren't known as Shadow Spirits, but as the Meoner; a very rich, very powerful people from Lestee. Some claim the map King Oden used to navigate to Henderbell was sent back across the Crystal Sea and given to them. It's said once they arrived in the shores of Henderbell, they led an attack against King Oden, but he used royal magic to defeat them, thus cursing them to be beasts for all eternity. That's the version we were taught."

"I'm assuming you know more about the story?" I asked.

"The elves found a scroll written by Vaneeries, their king at the time of their sailing. It spoke of a powerful magic also given to them. So powerful and dark they had to flee Meoner and ended up in Henderbell. They asked King Oden for help in settling in the new world, but the king discovered their magic and invited them to work with him."

"And that was a good thing?" I asked.

"For a while, until the king grew jealous of Vaneeries' influence over Henderbellians. He plotted to kill all who followed him. King Oden ordered the Henderbellian army to burn all of his followers at the stake on Christmas day, claiming they all committed treason." She sighed. "But magic can't be killed, only tamed."

"What do you mean?" My body stooped forward, my curiosity spiking.

"They didn't die," she replied. "They became what they are. Spirits that are neither living nor dead."

"What happened after?" I asked.

"King Oden called upon his sorcerers and witches, begging them to find a spell that could imprison them in the crypt beneath the castle in Ghenthar. And so they did," she continued. "But a more powerful magic set them free twenty-five years ago."

"What about the Soul Drainers?"

"They became extinct while Claudius the Fallen still ruled—at least that's what the history books say. But when the

Shadow Spirits returned twenty-five years ago, they brought them back."

"Maybe their magic lets them bring back the dead?" I suggested, frightened by my own comment.

"I don't think so," she said and continued, "The last time Ghenthar was attacked, Ishmael's parents died after imprisoning Vaneeries and his servants in the Prison of Krishmar."

"How come they didn't use a dagger like the one you have?"

"The blades made of Sacred Tears were discovered during the last attack," she answered. "There were too many of them and not enough time to forge more weapons. Now all weapons in Henderbell are made of them."

"Does anyone know how the Shadow Spirits found a way into Albernaith?" I asked.

"No," she replied. "We were told the magic of traveling between time and dimensions stayed with your family, but that can't be true." She reclined her head on the wall.

"And where does the connection between Henderbell and Earth come from?"

"Both worlds were created together. Beings with a higher conscience were placed in Henderbell and creatures of lower conscience on Albernaith—or Earth." She looked into my eyes, her golden locks falling over her face. "But creatures with a higher conscience were assigned the task to protect Albernaith."

"I don't think Henderbell has been doing a great job at that," I said with a scoff. "I mean, I'm not sure how much you know of that world, but it's a mess."

"Even if Albernaith was in order, your grandparents can't protect both worlds anymore, and your father and mother renounced the throne, abandoning Henderbellians and humans."

"At the end of the day, it's up to us to protect the ones we love." I reached for her hand. "Don't you agree?"

She shuddered at my touch.

"I think we do our best to keep them safe." Her words paved the way for a frown. "But most of the time, our best isn't enough." She slipped her hand away.

AVA

# CHAPTER 14

They probably thought I was asleep. I heard their entire conversation. I was glad Enzo found someone to talk to. He was always alone after his friends ditched him.

I stared at the ceiling as if it were a television. I guess a part of me hoped a Christmas movie would start playing at any moment. But even the magic of this world couldn't make that a reality.

I was looking forward to spending Christmas in Dorthcester since Mom brought it up. Honestly, I was relieved to be leaving the screaming behind for a couple of days. But I'd take their fights over all this talk of death.

Usually when I had nightmares, I'd hug Mr. Wombington, but he wasn't here. A part of me even believed he was responsible for all the beautiful dreams I had. I was pretty sure carrying him around gave people the impression I was more innocent than I looked. I enjoyed eavesdropping when people thought I wasn't listening.

After they wished each other good night, Enzo and Doopar returned to their beds. His loud snores began a few minutes later. I imagined how excited he was to actually be talking to an elf. Enzo had always been more of a dreamer than me. I could hear him in his room sometimes, making up dialogue for the characters he created on paper. He used to come up with books and comics and give them to me every week.

I shivered as a breeze touched my cheeks, blowing out all the candles around the room. I sat up on the bed and searched for whoever was responsible, my heart pounding fast. Did those creatures find a way in?

A blue speck of light appeared on the ceiling, moving like a hummingbird. My eyes followed it as it hovered above me.

I was about to scream when a deep voice said, "Don't be afraid."

"Who's there?" I whispered, burying half of my face under the covers.

"A friend," replied the voice as the light glistened.

All the beds in the room were suddenly empty, my surroundings growing dark until invisible.

"Where did they go?" I held a breath.

"They're sound asleep on their beds," said the voice, the blue light the only thing in view.

"But I can't see them."

"Reality isn't based on what you can see, sweet Ava." The light exploded into glitter, spreading above me like stars.

The darkness was replaced by a blue sky. Tall green trees sprung from a field of grass, suddenly covered by flowers colored like the rainbow. Birds flew above me, the flapping of their wings releasing a cloud of glowing dust. A waterfall was behind me, falling into a round lagoon. The air smelled like cinnamon buns on Christmas morning. Blue butterflies appeared, dancing around me while fluttering their purple wings.

I got up from my bed and smiled once the grass rubbed beneath my feet. The blue light appeared over my shoulder. It darted toward the woods and exploded into thousands of particles. White glares of light shaped like people appeared behind the trees, looking like ghosts with no faces, their bodies shiny and white.

An elk twice my size walked through the ghost people. Its golden coat shimmered as it approached me.

"I think I know who you are," I said with a sinking feeling in my stomach.

"And I know who *you* are, Ava." He was the owner of the voice. His mouth didn't move as he spoke.

"Kurah?"

"You caught me." He wiggled his ears. I sensed happiness in his voice.

"Am I still in Henderbell?" I really wanted to touch his shiny coat.

"Most definitely."

"But it looks so different."

"Just like seasons change, so does time." Kurah's voice made me feel peaceful. "The darkness you see has already been defeated in the future. You only need to water a seed to see a tree."

"You talk to me like I'm a grown up." I shrugged. "I'm just a girl."

"A brave girl who's witnessed more in nine years than many in their lives," he said.

"Technically I'm almost ten. My birthday is in February." A smile played on my lips. "And you think I'm brave?"

"The bravest almost-ten-year-old girl I know."

A cloud lifted from his antlers, flying in my direction. On its surface appeared a woman riding a horse, her body shielded by golden armor. She looked like my mom, but the brown eyes belonged to my dad. Her long dark hair was braided with a yellow ribbon. An army stood behind her as she held a sword in the air.

"Who is she?" I asked.

"You." His answer made my heart race. "I come from a place where time is a thought. There's only the now and in that place, you're not only a queen, but you're also a brave warrior."

"Can you travel in time and save my grandparents?" I asked, expecting a positive answer.

"I can't use time to delay or speed up your journey, sweet Ava. Only your actions can determine their fate." He raised his head, flapping his ears. "If I intrude when uninvited, I may save a life, but I may also damage the future."

"How's that possible?" I watched the woman—well, me—on the cloud, observing my reflection on her armor.

"Time is what every living creature needs to evolve," he said as the images changed, showing the warrior woman wearing a long purple dress, a silver crown on her head, and a scepter in her hand, its tip shaped like the twisted branches of a tree. She looked at me and smiled.

"Can she see me?" I asked, eyes wide.

"No," he answered.

"Why didn't you call my brother, too?" I stretched out my hand, trying to touch the woman, but it was like catching a cloud.

"He isn't the seed Henderbell needs right now. You are, Ava." The images disappeared. "Enzo needs to believe again. You must tell them I came to you."

"Me?" His words confused me. "You want me to tell them I saw you? Aren't you, like, the most powerful god in Henderbell?"

His lips curved into what I assumed was a smile. "That's exactly why you were chosen to see me."

"Because I'm a weak girl?" The trees behind him moved with the wind.

"A heart that can believe is never weak." He huffed as he stepped closer to me.

"What if they don't believe me?"

He lowered his head, his dark eyes meeting mine. "Then you will. I only need one seed to see a grown tree."

"Since time works differently where you're from, can you see the future?" I asked.

"I can see many futures," he replied.

"What do you mean?"

"Every living being is given the opportunity to choose their fate. Their future is built upon their choices."

"Will we save my grandparents?" I asked, afraid of his answer.

"Yes and no." He frowned. It was a strange thing to see an elk frown its forehead.

"I don't get it."

"You may save them if you choose that path, but you may also let them die if you choose another. The choice is yours."

"Then I believe we'll save them."

"Then let it be in Henderbell as it is in your heart. But remember, it isn't enough to believe. You need to act upon it," he said as silver sparkles appeared around his antlers. The forest started melting like ice, the walls of the hideaway appearing again.

"Are you leaving?" I asked, alarmed as the darkness thinned.

"Yes and no." His body became golden dust, floating up in the air. "I could never leave you."

I was back in the hideaway, sitting on my bed. Enzo was asleep beside me, Ishmael and Doopar on the other side.

Was it all a dream? Did I really see Kurah?

A blue light shone from the comforter on the bed, the ornament Barthemeus gave me being the source. My fingers traced its antlers, the image of Kurah's face in my head.

I laid on my pillow and held the ornament in my hand until falling asleep.

# ISHMAEL

# CHAPTER 15

Everyone was still asleep when my eyes fluttered open. The place was quiet, the candles still burning. The smell of bread and freshly brewed coffee lingered. I wish I hadn't woken up from my dream. Loomstak and I had fled Ghenthar and built a life away from the city. We lived in a cabin surrounded by greenery and animals. There was no talk of war or pain, no laws reminding us we weren't allowed to love one another. His lavender eyes glistened with joy. Even in my dreams, the reflection of the sun against his silver hair sent my heart to a race.

Why did I send him to the Prison? I wish I had fought harder for us. I questioned the reason why I was so reluctant to approach the king about such laws. Perhaps I didn't love him as

A tear fell down my cheek onto the pillow, regret a sudden companion.

"Why are you crying?" I was startled by the sight of Ava standing at the foot of my bed, wearing her grandma's old pink coat over her yellow blouse.

"Sorry, princess," I sat up, wiping my eyes with a wrist, "did I wake you?"

"I didn't sleep much," she whispered with a smirk.

"I, on the other hand, was having a wonderful dream."

"You talked when you were dreaming. You must really love him."

My chest lifted with a frayed breath. "Are you hungry?" I grabbed my boots from the side of my bed, put them on, and walked to the shelf with the bread.

"You said you were afraid." She sat on a chair by the table.

"I did?" I scoffed, grabbing the warm loaf from the shelf.

"What are you afraid of?" Her eyes followed my every move, watching me put the bread on the table.

"We don't have enough time for me to answer that question," I replied.

"Maybe you don't want to find the time to answer it."

"You're young in years but wise in words, princess." I returned to the shelf and grabbed a jar full of water and a few cups. "I guess the only thing the magic surrounding this place can bake is bread."

"It's okay." She took a slice.

I sat across from her. She stared as if I was a rare jewel.

"Thank you for taking good care of my brother and me," she said with a mouth full of food.

"Yeah, thank you." Enzo wobbled his way toward us, rubbing his eyes. Doopar followed, her hair up in a ponytail. Both joined us at the table. We ate in silence. I assumed all were haunted by the same thoughts I was. We were only five days away from Christmas and there was still no sign of the king and the queen.

"What are we going to do?" Doopar gulped the water in her cup. "We can't just stay cooped up in this place eating bread."

"I know, I know." I buried my face in the palm of my hands. "We need to go there."

"Go where?" Doopar frowned.

"The Prison of Krishmar," I replied.

"I thought about that too but it's too risky, especially with Enzo and Ava."

"Do you have any other suggestions?" I asked. "You scouted many locations with Loomstak. I'm open to any other ideas."

Her brows were released from her frown. She ran her hand over her face and said, "No."

"Why is everyone so afraid of this prison?" Enzo asked, fingers tapping on the table.

"None were ever allowed inside," I replied. "King Nicholas said the magic used to contain the Shadow Spirits was too dark and powerful for anyone, but especially elves. A law was even established emphasizing all of this."

"But didn't you send an army of elves there before we arrived?" Enzo scowled.

"I did." A sinking feeling wrapped around my chest. "And they never returned."

Enzo turned to Doopar with a look of concern. "So if you go, *you* might not come back."

"There's no other alternative," she mentioned.

Enzo's shoulders drooped down, lips parted.

"What do you believe, Ishmael?" Ava asked, fingers laced on the table.

Enzo stared at his sister, surprised at her question.

"Princess, I'm not sure what you mean," I said.

"Do you think we'll win this battle?" She placed a hand over mine. "Do you think we'll find them?"

What answer could I give the nine-year-old granddaughter of my king and queen? What response could I provide that wouldn't trigger fear in her innocent heart?

"All we need is a seed to see a tree," she continued. "Your feelings are seeds."

"What happened to you?" Wrinkles carved on Enzo's forehead.

She smiled. "Kurah came to me last night."

I retrieved my hand away from her touch.

"How's that possible?" Doopar asked. "He hasn't been seen in hundreds of years."

"You mean the elk from that story?" Enzo scoffed. "Are you sure you weren't dreaming or something?"

"I'm pretty sure, Enzo," she said, displeased at her brother's question. "He said the darkness we see has been defeated where he lives." Her smile remained intact. "Then he showed me the future and I was a queen."

Doopar tilted her head and folded her arms. "What was the color of his coat?"

Ava's head jerked back with a look of surprise. "Gold," she said after a brief silence. "It was so bright. His eyes were dark and round."

"Incredible," Doopar mumbled. "It couldn't have been a dream. She can't be making this up."

"How do you know?" Enzo questioned, using one of the legs of the table as support for his foot as he leaned back on his chair.

"She was never told Kurah's coat was made of gold," I answered. "She must've really seen him."

"Did he say anything else?" Doopar asked.

"That what matters is what we believe in our hearts, not what we see," she said.

"So he's a liar," Enzo barked, his chair dropping back to its place. "Definitely not interested in meeting this animal."

"What's gotten into you?" Doopar shook her head. "Were you bitten by a bug this morning?"

"The bug of foolishness." He sneered at his sister. "Ava, it was obviously a dream. I mean, why would he come to you? You're just a kid who still thinks her teddy bear talks to her."

"What's that supposed to mean?" Ava pursed her lips. "Just because I'm a kid I'm stupid?"

"I just don't want you to be disappointed by believing some magical creature you saw in a dream."

"How can you say that after the past few days?" Ava contested. "We've done nothing but breathe magic. How can you not believe me of all people?"

Enzo darted up his feet. "You know how many times I believed Mom and Dad were going to be together? You know how many times I wished those stupid kids from school away? But it never happened. Instead, we're here, stuck in this place, and apparently we're all going to disappear in a couple of days. If what the animal said was true, none of this would've happened. We'd be home, part of a happy family. But we are not."

"Shut up!" Ava banged her hands on the table. "You aren't the only one who knows things."

"I know more than you. Why do you think I'd stay with you in your room when they started arguing?" Enzo said, the veins on his neck visible beneath his skin.

"We could still hear them," she said. "And I'd pretend I wasn't listening so you wouldn't feel bad."

"Good to know. At least you know life isn't a fairytale, and just when we found one, it turned out to be a nightmare."

"He said he didn't call you because you couldn't see him." Ava's eyes glistened. "Because you needed to believe on what was good again. Maybe this was your chance to believe in something, and you blew it."

Enzo walked away from the table and sat on the edge of his bed, eyes on the ground.

"What do you believe, Ava?" Doopar asked. Enzo shifted his gaze toward his sister.

"We'll find them," she said in a broken voice. "Christmas is hope, isn't it? If we lose hope in our hearts, we've already destroyed Christmas and our world."

"The girl speaking in front of me has gained wisdom beyond her years," I said. "Hold on to that hope. We need it more than ever."

"Ishmael, you're certain no one knows of this hideaway?" Doopar asked, her posture rigid.

"Unless the king and queen revealed it to someone," I answered. "But as far as I know, no one knows it's here."

"Then they'll be safe," Doopar declared. "We should go to the prison and face whatever magic lingers inside its walls."

"But it's too dangerous," Enzo said, walking toward Doopar.

"It's more dangerous for Ishmael and I to stay cooped up here," Doopar admonished. "We need to keep on looking. You're the offspring of Saint Nicholas. You need to stay here. We can't lose you two, so…"

"But we're going to be alone," Ava said.

"This is the safest place you could be, princess," I said. "And you're with your brother. You'll be alright."

"Big deal." She waved her hand in dismissal. "He doesn't believe anything I say apparently."

Doopar's eyes fixed on Enzo. "I'm sure he'll come to his senses."

I opened one of the drawers from the cabinet beneath the shelves and took out a rolled parchment paper and a compass. I unrolled it on the table, revealing a map of Henderbell.

"If we don't return in two days," I started. "Then I need you to go here." I pointed to the symbol of the skull crowned with thorns on the northwest part of the map. "This is the Prison of Krishmar. It's located on the edge of the cliff." I handed Enzo the compass. "Use the compass. It'll show you the way."

He clutched his hand around the object and turned to Doopar. "What if one of those things finds you?"

"It's a risk I'll have to take. I can't let Ishmael go alone, and you both need to stay here. We can't risk your exposure," she said. "Your lives are more valuable than ours. I'm just an elf. He's just a man. There are plenty more like us."

"I highly doubt that," Enzo said.

"But what if the Shadow Spirits are there?" Ava asked.

"Then you'll have to find a way to remain unseen." My words paled their faces.

Doopar approached the set of armors aligned on the wall. She surveyed them until one captured her full attention. It was made of bronze with tree branches carved on its chest plate, the patterns outlined in red and gold. The helmet was shaped like an elk's head, its antlers resembling crooked branches.

"Is this the sacred armor of Delier?" She touched the hilt of a sword clinging to a belt pinned to the wall.

"Yes," I said. "I was actually surprised you didn't recognize it yesterday. Didn't you read hundreds of books on her?"

"I sure did." She turned to the armor and stared as if it was a rare creature. "My father told me her story. She inspired me to hone my fighting skills. She sailed with King Oden—the first elven woman to be a warrior." She extended her hand and grabbed the sword, the scabbard, and the belt. "She was the one to cut off the head of Claudius the Fallen."

"And lost hers right after," I added.

She scrunched her face. "Loyalty can get you killed."

"I hope her sword serves you well." I approached the silver armor next to her. Antlers rose from its guard-braces, the armor's surface covered in thin purple lines forming the shape of many faces. Its breastplate was a deep blue, a silver Henderbellian sigil at the center, surrounded by two elks.

"And whose was this?" Ava was behind me.

"Julius Rose," I replied. "Your great uncle. When your grandparents got married, your grandmother moved from Rosethorn, the kingdom of the south, to Ghenthar. Her brother accompanied her and died when the Shadow Spirits last attacked twenty-five years ago."

"Was he a good fighter?" Ava observed her reflection on the armor.

"Incredible actually," I replied, retrieving the sword, its scabbard, and the belt beside it. "He was funny too. He used to share jokes and stories when I was a kid."

I fixed the belt around my waist, Doopar following my act.

"You're leaving now?" Ava asked with an edge.

"We can't waste any more time," Doopar affirmed. "We have to go. We have to walk since I can't risk attracting any Shadow Spirits or Soul Drainers."

"Okay." Ava's lips curved into a half-hearted smile. "Be careful."

"I will," Doopar said and turned to Enzo.

"Promise you'll come back," he said.

"I won't promise something I may not keep." Her words earned a frown from him. "What I can promise is that I'll try my best to save your kin, Henderbell, and Ghenthar."

"That'll be enough. For now," he said.

"I'll see you, princess," I said, my head turning to Enzo. "Two days. Don't forget."

"Alright," he whispered.

The shape of the elk's head appeared above us once we stood by the stairs, the trees visible on the other side.

# CHAPTER 16

Not a single cloud obstructed the view of the blue sky. The mountain peaks covered in a white blanket emerged behind the tree line. Snow crunched under our feet with our every step. The tree barks in the Forest of Nick were a dull gray. Many claimed the trees lost their color due to a curse placed in these woods. The only trees that remained green were the pines.

These parts were quiet, animals avoided it. The vegetation was old and would probably share dark tales if it could speak.

The long eerie silence was the spark my mind needed to fuel unwanted memories. The dead have a way of reminding us how temporary we are. But right now, the memories were claws of guilt and failure, ensnaring me at the thought the Shadow Spirits and Soul Drainers had returned under *my* watch—a reminder that the death of my parents meant nothing. It also meant I had failed those who had taken me in when I became an orphan. Though I tried to push away the darkness in my mind, my guilt was greater than peace.

Doopar was ahead of me, observing our surroundings like a predator watching its prey.

I knew she was special the first time we met. We were young and naive. Her father and mother also died when the Shadow Spirits attacked.

After spending some time with my thoughts, I was surprised by the sight of a cardania tree riddled with fruit. Its branches were twisted like scraggly roots tied together, the round blue fruits hanging at their tips.

"Well, look here!" I said. "This is a nice surprise."

I plucked two fruits and tossed one to Doopar.

"When I was a kid," I started, "my father and I would venture into the woods near Ghenthar to find these around Christmas. We'd pick as many as we could so mother could bake a cake."

"Why do you think Henderbell was kept a secret from them?" Doopar bit into the cardania, a yellow streak of the fruit's juice running down the corner of her mouth.

"I can tell you were very interested in my story." I smirked and sunk my teeth into the fruit's smooth surface.

"Sorry." She wiped her lips with a wrist. "I've been thinking about that since I found them. I could understand them keeping the grandkids a secret, but why hide Henderbell from them? They aren't ordinary humans born in the human realm. They're Griffins. Imagine if we hadn't known about them. We would've probably had them arrested."

"I'm not sure why they preferred to hide the truth," I replied. "Maybe they wanted to protect their innocence."

"Ishmael, they're from Albernaith." Doopar pressed her lips into a line, a nod of disapproval followed. "How innocent can they be? You remember the stories we heard. Look at how broken they are."

"I can see why you like Enzo." Her eyes widened at my words. "You like fixing things and he needs a lot of work."

"I wouldn't say I like him," she said. "I find him interesting."

"In the same way your mother found his father interesting?"

She took another bite from the cardania and shifted her gaze to the vegetation. "When I was a child, he'd come over to see my mother and me when my father wasn't home." Emptiness took her eyes. "At the time, elves could still only live in the outskirts of Ghenthar. The law didn't allow us to live in the city."

"I remember."

"A part of me knew what they were doing wasn't right, but he actually paid attention to what I had to say, even if I was three years old. Though my father always loved me, there was something about Bane that drew me. I never questioned my mother about him. I was too afraid of her answer. And I was afraid he was going to leave us if I did ask." She took in a long breath. "I remember when I found my mom weeping, sitting alone at our table with a piece of paper in hand."

"What was on it?" I asked.

"The drawing Enzo had with him when I found them," she replied. "It was a farewell gift from Bane to me. He never came back to the house. My mother never saw him again. I'm still wondering how Enzo found it."

"I'm sorry."

"There's nothing to be sorry for." She caressed the cardania with her thumb. "My mother was the one having an affair with Bane while my father was away. She sowed that seed, watered that tree, and reaped its fruit."

"At least Enzo is alone and sixteen in human years." I smirked.

"You know better than anyone what it means to be human and love an elf." Her words made my stomach churn. "My mother was a past time for Bane. I don't see how I could be different for his son. He was young and probably craved adventure beyond the walls of the castle. She craved company and he fulfilled her needs."

"Enzo wasn't raised here," I reminded her. "None of them were brought up as royalty. Their hearts know nothing of ruling and kingdoms. Perhaps that's why Kurah chose Ava to see him."

"Maybe that's why they were never told of Henderbell." Doopar tossed away whatever was left of the cardania. "So their hearts wouldn't lust after power."

"Here's a bit of advice," I said. "Whatever you want to do or say, do it so you won't be filled with regret." Our eyes locked. "Life gave me Loomstak, and yet I worried more about titles than about loving him." A knot built in my throat. "If we survive this, I'll ask him to marry me and even if King Nicholas refuses to change our laws, I'll still do it."

"But you'd be exiled," she said.

"I'll run away," I revealed, my stomach fluttering at the thought. "Go to Lestee. Leave it all behind. Now that the grandchildren are here, I don't see much use for me. It's only a matter of time until Enzo is old enough to rule."

"You don't even know if he wants it," she contested.

"Ever heard of a man who didn't love power?" My eyes narrowed.

"No," she whispered.

"And if he doesn't want it, Ava will. You saw the look on her face when she sat on that throne. It's in their blood whether they like it or not."

My teeth sunk into the cardania as I reclined my shoulder on a tree, arms folded over my chest. I winced as the pin of the Henderbellian sigil prickled at my skin. I removed it from my chest and tossed it on the ground.

"What are you doing?" she asked, face shrouded in surprise.

"Resigning." I imagined the contagious smile that would cross Loomstak's face once I broke the news.

"I need to ask you something." Doopar's voice trembled. "If a Soul Drainer takes hold of me again, and you see no hope of it leaving my body, I need you to kill me."

The fruit fell out of my hand. "Don't say that."

"Promise me," she insisted. "I don't want to die at their hands, Ishmael."

"You won't."

"You can't promise that," she said. "But you can promise me that you'll spare me if that fate finds me."

"I promise," I said with a shudder.

# CHAPTER 17

We carried on, silence a companion for the both of us. After a few hours, the rays of the sun turned to wisps in the darkening sky. The trees were exchanged by a clearing, gray boulders protruding out of the snow; to the left a cliff and a view of the surrounding mountains covered in ice. Ahead was a moat of stone, at its end the Prison of Krishmar. Its walls were as dark as a crow's feather, covered in leafless branches and twigs. The prison had been built on a lonely rock, the stone moat being the only bridge between the ground and its entrance. It was shaped like a square with a tower in the middle, the top a triangle. At the center of the tower was the sigil of Krishmar: the skull crowned with thorns.

The macabre sight stirred fear in me. What were we going to find inside? Were Loomstak and the other elves being kept within its walls? Did they have King Nicholas and Queen Mary in there?

The wind blew across the clearing, lifting a cloud of snow. All the stories I heard about this place haunted me as we approached the macabre sight.

The tales of the prison spoke of an evil dwelling behind its walls even before the Shadow Spirits were imprisoned. It spoke of a group that rebelled under the reign of King Oden. The rebels known as Krishmarians served Claudius the Fallen and didn't take well to their new king after he was defeated. They raided towns and villages, killing all in sight. They claimed to be vessels for blood magic, always seeking to expand their knowledge. Rumors spread that they had a secret hideaway to host their meetings. Henderbellian soldiers searched, trying to find them, until they stumbled upon this place and found their bodies scattered across the clearing and inside the prison's walls. Every single corpse had a hole in their chest, their hearts missing. Many claimed their magic kept this place invisible to the naked eye until all were killed.

I leaned over as we crossed the stone moat, the chasm below covered by a mist. Stars appeared in the sky as the last rays of the sun struggled to shine.

We halted in front of the double iron doors, bones carved on their bronze surfaces. Their edges were covered by stubs shaped like thorns. I tried pushing them open with my shoulder, but they remained still.

"How do we enter this place?" My eyes followed up the tower.

Golden strings silently shot up from the top of the tower, spreading across the sky like fireworks. A golden dome formed around the prison as the sigil of the thorn-crowned skull in the middle of the tower was engulfed by light.

The doors creaked open, revealing nothing but darkness on the other side.

It was as if I had my eyes closed once I crossed through the doorway. Every step echoed as if I was inside an empty room. But the darkness didn't last long. It thinned like rising smoke, revealing a wide empty hall. The ground was of pure white marble, the walls hidden behind a whirling gray mist. The Krishmarian symbol was displayed across the entire ceiling, carved out of gold. A faint light shone from it, illuminating the eerie structure.

The mist on the wall to the right slithered on the ground like a snake, approaching Doopar and me. It danced in the air and shot up to the ceiling, covering the symbol, revealing doors scattered around us.

The sound of creaking hinges crawled in my ears.

A shadow shaped like a man emerged to my right, wobbling closer, arms stretched wide. His body was cloaked, the fabric stained with blood splatters. A sinking feeling took my stomach at the image of his bruised face. His eyes were surrounded by dark circles, his hair tangled.

"Bane?" I whispered.

"Impossible," Doopar quivered.

"Help me," he begged. "Please, don't leave me. They won't let me go."

"That's not him," Doopar mentioned. "That can't be him."

"It's me. Please, don't leave me," he insisted, rushing his steps. "Don't leave me here to rot. My children…Evelyn…"

His jaw widened as he screamed. The louder the sound, the wider it grew, his skin ripping like paper. His body exploded into dust, flying toward the ceiling and disappearing into the Krishmarian sigil.

"An elf," echoed a menacing voice.

"Yes, yes, an elf," said another.

"They'll be pleased."

"Very pleased."

"Who's there?" Doopar shouted, unsheathing her sword. "Who's there?"

"Look at her. Look at her. Look at…" The voices faded away.

Tormented screams erupted.

Doopar dropped her weapon and covered her ears. I cringed at the sound. The suffering voices of men, women, and children turned into a haunting symphony. I fell to my knees, my heart racing faster as the screams grew louder.

Sudden silence.

"Doopar?" I moaned.

"I'm here," she said weakly.

Darkness surrounded me, but it was soon pierced by a thin glowing line. It moved like a hummingbird, forming the shape of a door.

Doopar retrieved her sword from the ground as I rose to my feet. We slowly walked toward the strange sight. It opened as we drew nearer, revealing stone walls lit by a burning torch on the other side.

My lips slowly broke into a smile. Here he was, covered in a ragged dark cloak, body bruised, his white beard stained with blood. He laid on the ground, wrists and ankles chained, the smell of putrid flesh lingering. Seeing him was like drawing poison from a wound.

He lifted his gaze. "Ishmael? Doopar? How?" A weak smile crossed his chapped lips, his beard untrimmed, hair resembling a bird's nest.

"King Nicholas!" I wrapped my arms around him.

"My boy," he laughed weakly.

"Are you hurt?" I asked, cupping his face between my hands, his skin cold. "Are you alright?"

"I can tell you everything once we get out of here," he said with tears in his eyes.

"It's good to see you, my king," Doopar said with a frown.

"A brave elf. Breaking the law to follow a friend."

Her face grew rigid.

"Where's the queen?" I asked.

A downcast look shrouded his face. "I haven't seen her since they brought me here," he replied, his breath a foul smell. "We need to find her. They keep asking about my grandchildren. Have you seen them? Are they safe?"

"They're in Henderbell. They're safe," I said proudly. I may have failed at many other things, but I had kept his offspring alive.

"Are they protected?" He narrowed his brown eyes.

"They're at the hideaway in the Forest of Nick. They found a way into Henderbell on their own. They're fine."

A tear streaked down his cheek. "Does anyone else know they're there?"

"No," I replied. "We took them there yesterday."

"Good." He chuckled. "Good."

The door slammed shut. A pungent smell invaded my nostrils as maggots appeared over King Nicholas' face and arms, spreading throughout his body. His skin melted, dripping on the floor like water, leaving a skeleton in plain sight.

I stood frozen and confused. Doopar stared, despair in her eyes.

My surroundings faded, the empty hall now in view once again, every wall covered by a layer of gray mist moving like the waves of ocean, crashing onto each other. The sigil on the roof throbbed in a faint a light.

Footsteps echoed from my right. I held up my sword; Doopar repeated my act. I followed the sound. The shape of a man emerged from behind the mist on the wall. He walked with determined steps. As he approached, I recognized the broken armor shielding his body. The Henderbellian symbol on his breastplate glistened once the light touched his mangled face.

"It's one of Loomstak's men," Doopar said in a trembling voice.

A long gash spread between his brows and lower right cheek. He had a hole for one of his eyes, his silver hair wisps falling over his face. The tip of one of his ears was mutilated, streaks of blood surrounding the wound, spreading to his neck.

"What have they done to him?" she asked.

More footsteps joined. More shadows appeared from behind the mist. Their bodies a canvas for bruises, their armors shattered remains covering their bodies. The smell of rotten flesh filled the room.

They surrounded us, an army of elven corpses. Their lacerated faces were a reminder that Loomstak might be among them. They wheezed, eyes set on us.

"You were drawn to me like a predator to its prey," affirmed a guttural voice.

A wisp of cloud appeared from the Krishmarian symbol in the ceiling, twirling its way down. Its shape shifted once touching the ground. His upper body was exposed, an X-shaped scar streaked across his chest. Three horns protruded from his bald head, the middle one smaller than the others. He wore brown pants covered in tears and holes, dark boots smudged with blood stains.

"I must praise your courage to enter this place," he continued in a snide tone. His eyes were of a light gray color, making them almost entirely white. "But none of you should be praised for your foolishness." He puckered his lips. "Ishmael, I thought you knew your king better. To believe he'd be handed to you like that…" He sighed. "That would've made this game far too simple."

"Game?" My muscles tensed.

"Oh, yes, one I enjoy playing very much," he replied.

"You're Vaneeries, the king of the Shadow Spirits." My sword was pointed at him.

"Please." He sniggered. "You think the lord of the Shadow Spirits would linger here out of all places? He's preparing his own Christmas festivities. I'm but a servant fulfilling his orders."

"Do you have a name?" Doopar asked.

"I can feel your power," he said, smelling the air. "You're no ordinary elf, are you?"

"She asked you a question," I said.

A chuckle. "Lower your weapon and you'll get an answer. Honestly, who enters someone's home and demands things like that?"

Doopar raised a hand, a sphere of white light forming on her palm.

"I wouldn't do that if I were you." He smiled, revealing a set of yellowed teeth. "Unless you want to be taken again."

The sphere of light receded.

"Can we talk like civilized people?" His arms spread out with a shrug.

"You're challenging my patience," I said.

"What did you think was going to happen by coming here?" He strolled around us, hands crossed behind his back. "Did you think you were going to be handed what you wanted?" He halted. "When I got word that an elven army was marching toward the prison, I immediately knew only a fool would've sent them here. I kept wondering who was left to rule after King Nicholas and Queen Mary disappeared. The purple shade of your robes have provided an answer."

Silence.

"And to answer your question," he continued. "My name is Molock, one of the Specters of Vaneeries. And we have returned to avenge our history."

"It's your third attempt to do that," Doopar said. "You failed twenty-five years ago. You failed when you first arrived in these lands, and you'll fail again."

"Says the elf as if her kind was born in Henderbell." Molock smirked. "Your people will go extinct. Elves will be but a memory in the minds of those who survive what's about to come."

A dead soldier stole Doopar's sword from her grasp as Molock ensnared her cheeks, pulling her closer. My arms were grabbed by two soldiers, their stench a trigger for tears. My sword escaped my grasp and thudded on the ground as I struggled to break free.

"Look at him and see what you'll become." He grabbed the nape of her neck, holding her face inches away from one of the dead elven soldiers. She tried to look away. "Look at him!" he shouted, using his other hand to pull her hair, forcing her gaze to meet the corpse. He had no eyes, dry blood streaks stained his cheeks, ears mutilated. "Soul Drainers are inside of every single one of them. They've been perfected to fulfill a purpose much greater than their own."

"You killed them all?" I asked.

"Only those I didn't need." He puckered his lips. "It's no fun killing all of them. Those I needed were kept half alive to the point the Soul Drainers could use their memories to infiltrate places I needed." He swung Doopar by her neck, releasing her to one of the corpses. But before the dead elf could ensnare her, she reached into her boots and retrieved the dagger. As she raised the weapon toward Molock, he twitched his head right, her wrist twisting at his movement. She cringed, dropping her dagger on the ground, the weapon retrieved by one of the elven corpses.

"You have some guts, elf!" Wrinkles appeared on Molock's forehead.

One of the dead elves grabbed Doopar's arms, the veins on her neck in view, her eyes locked on Molock.

"Maybe I'll kill you once a Soul Drainer takes you again." He chuckled. "Maybe I'll let you watch those you love die. Still deciding."

Rage spread down my body.

Sand poured from the Krishmarian symbol above me, pilling on the ground, each grain moving like ants. They formed two piles, each one taking the shape of a living nightmare. They stood taller than me, no eyes, lips thin and long. Branches grew out of their heads, lacing into a thorn-covered crown, their upper bodies shielded by a rusty breastplate. The two Shadow Spirits wheezed, bodies stooped forward.

"Thank you, by the way, for giving away the location of the hideaway. I must admit, I'm a bit disappointed you didn't let us play hide and seek with them a little longer." Molock removed a vile filled with blood from one of his pockets, turned to the Shadow Spirits and said, "When you find the hideaway, pour this blood over the soil. Only royal blood can unveil the location. Find the kids. Bring them to me. Lay down your lives if needed."

Molock raised a hand toward me, his fingers spread out. Particles of dust shot out from his palm, invading my nostrils.

My vision blurred.

My legs grew weak.

Darkness.

# ENZO

# CHAPTER 18

Ava and I had taken to books instead of speaking ever since they left. It was hard to tell if it was light or dark outside since there were no windows in the hideaway.

While looking through the shelf, I picked up *Mockery, Flattery, and Magic* by Tardum Ovenee, a collection of Henderbellian fairytales. It was the most interesting title I found. I thought about reading the book on the Shadow Spirits Doopar read last night, but I was tired of thinking about those creatures.

I sat beside the bookshelf, in the same spot Doopar and I spent some time last night. From the corner of my eye, I spotted the title of Ava's book: *The Battle of Hope*. She had been reading that book since their departure.

My attention shifted from the yellowed pages to my sister, who sat on her bed, legs crossed. In her hand was the ornament shaped like the Henderbellian sigil. I watched her read in her yellow long sleeve and scarlet boots. So much in her reminded me of my grandmother.

"I'm sorry." I closed the book on my lap.

"For?" Ava's gaze remained on the pages in front of her.

I rolled my eyes. "I bet you thought everyone was going to doubt you—everyone but me."

"I thought no one was going to believe me," she revealed. "But I thought you were going to give me a chance, at least. I mean, after all we've lived in the past few days."

"I know. You gave all my stories a chance back home."

"And *those* were made up." She shrugged. "I don't blame you for what you said. But you didn't even try to believe me."

"I'm sorry," I said.

"Don't worry." She smirked. "You're still on my good list."

"You're not angry?"

"At what?" She tossed the book on the bed. "At you?"

I sniggered. "Well, that too." I approached her and sat on the bed, book in hand. "Aren't you angry we're in this situation? We didn't ask for it. Any of it. It just sort of happened. One day we were Enzo and Ava, and the next, Prince Enzo and Princess Ava, heirs to the throne of Henderbell."

"We didn't ask for our parents, but we have them. We didn't ask for our breath, but we have it. We make the best of it. Can you try to make the best of this?"

"Where's my sister and what have you done to her?" I asked.

"She's here." She fixed her hair behind her ears. "She just decided to speak more. I think it'll be good for people. Especially after reading this book. I'll probably read more before bed now. Mr. Wombington used to tell me all kinds of stories."

"You miss him?" I asked.

"So much," she said. "He was a good friend."

The fact she still spoke of Mr. Wombington as if the bear was a living being just made me more aware of how innocent she was.

I smiled. "So what was he like?"

"Mr. Wombington?" She scrunched her face.

I laughed. "No, Kurah."

"So beautiful! He was big, his body was gold and shiny. His voice was so peaceful. It was crazy. He showed myself as queen!" she squealed. "He said it was the future. I was in armor, riding a white horse. I had a sword and there was an army behind me."

Her response sent shivers down my body.

"So you were in battle?" I asked. "Why else would you have an army behind you?"

"As *queen*. Can you focus on the positive?"

"I promise to try."

"Good," she said. "Anyway, it was amazing. I guess I'll be learning sword fighting."

"So you want to stay here?" I feared her answer.

A smile slowly unrolled on her face. "I could see myself living here. We were made for so much more than what we have back home."

I couldn't disagree with her.

"If Kurah showed you a vision of yourself in armor with a sword in hand and an army, this also means you'll go to war," I said. "That doesn't scare you?"

"Not really." Her smile became a line. "We're at war now. We need to sow good seeds so a good tree can grow."

"Apparently once you've seen Kurah, you develop a special love for gardening and plants."

"You're silly." She sniggered and continued, "How do you feel about being here?"

"You mean, how do I feel about waiting for the end of the world?"

"No, I'm serious. Pretend like we arrived in Henderbell at a time when Grandma and Grandpa were on the throne, and there was no talk of death or war." Her chin rested on her hands, elbows on her knees. "How would you have felt about this place?"

"I'd hope to feel like I belonged. Right now I feel like an outcast," I replied.

"That'll go away when you see him," Ava said proudly. "You know, it says here Kurah and Hambeon fought for almost a hundred years. Isn't that crazy?"

"That's intense." I jumped to my feet. "Let me put this book back. I've been reading it for hours. I need something new."

A growl pierced the atmosphere while I walked to the shelf.

"What was that?" Ava asked.

A hair-raising screech followed.

"I think it's them," I whispered, heart sinking into my chest. "The Shadow Spirits."

"They can't get in here. We're protected by magic." Color abandoned her face. "Right?"

"Quiet." The stone steps held my attention. My limbs trembled as the ground turned as clear as glass. They were at the entrance of the hideaway, hands smeared in blood, chests hidden under their rusty armor. Doopar's words were suddenly a blaring voice in my head: *Even magic can be tricked.*

I rushed to the set of armors lined up against the wall and grabbed one of the swords, the weapon so heavy, my arms trembled.

"What are you doing?" Ava begged.

"Just hide under the bed."

Ava did as I asked. I joined her, weapon in hand.

They snarled as they walked down the steps, arms dangling at their sides. Every wheezing breath wrapped me in fear and despair. My grasp tightened around the sword's handle as my eyes followed their every move. Their long thin lips curved into a smile as they strolled around. Their faces were carved with holes for eyes, and a crown of thorns sat on their heads.

Ava pressed a hand over her mouth, chest heaving, tears rolling down her flushed cheeks.

One of them approached the set of armors lined up on the wall, sniffed them and brought one down, the pieces clattering on the floor.

My chest tightened around my lungs.

The other walked toward the bed while its companion disappeared into the bathroom. Ava whimpered as the footsteps of the creature got louder, its boots smeared in blood.

It stood still.

Silence settled.

The bed shook until raised above us, thrown over the table and breaking into pieces.

Ava screamed.

The Shadow Spirit extended its arms, leaning closer, its lips pulled into an eerie smile.

This was it.

We were going to be taken.

But even if struggling with trembling arms, I raised the sword and plunged the blade into its chest.

A frightening screech followed my act.

It fumbled back, the sword still stuck in its body. I grabbed Ava by the wrist, pulled her up and ran to the stairs. Loud thuds and howls followed as we darted up the stone steps.

The frigid air struck my cheeks. I looked back while running toward the trees, the other Shadow Spirit in pursuit.

"Don't look back!" I shouted amidst heavy breaths, holding tightly to her hand.

My eyes were set on the forest as we ran through the snow, the sky stained with an orange hue as the sun set.

We jumped over rock and bark after entering the tree line. Every shadow casted by the fading light of day was perceived by my mind as one of the creatures.

Branches rustled above us. It was up on the trees, leaping from branch to branch like a monkey. But at the sound of a squeal, the creature turned around and headed toward the hideaway.

We kept on running.

My throat burned.

Ava wheezed, cheeks red.

I spotted a cave to my right, its entrance surrounded by trees and vines. We rushed inside, the last rays of the sun providing somewhat of a view. A clear layer of ice stretched over the rock formations on the wall; stalactites hung from the ceiling, the ground black dirt.

I reclined my back on an iceless gap on the wall, the rough surface brushing my shoulder. My chest heaved as my lungs clawed for breath. Ava sat on a rock while scanning our surroundings.

I sat on the ground, my pulse pounding in my ears.

Ava joined me at my side.

"Think...we...lost it?" she asked behind chattering teeth.

"I think...so. Try not...to speak."

Every breath was like a dagger ripping through my throat.

"It's so...cold," Ava moaned. "So cold..."

My chest lifted. "Try not to think about it. Even breaths, come on."

She followed my breathing pattern.

We held on to each other, my mind haunted by the truth: returning to the hideaway wasn't an option, and staying in this freezing cave meant certain death.

# CHAPTER 19

Ava and I crawled deeper into the cave due to a piercing breeze creeping inside. We left our coats behind and the freezing temperature made me fully aware our clothes weren't going to protect us for long. I didn't want to go too far so we'd have some source of light for the night. But once the sun set, the faint light of the winter moon wasn't enough to illuminate the darkness.

Ava and I shivered, holding on to each other. At least the shivers meant we were still alive.

Anger spread down body. I didn't ask to be in this situation. I never wished to find this place and fight its wars. I just wanted a glimpse of a normal life—whatever that meant. My mind reminded me of the comforts of home: my bed, my vinyl collection, my sketchbook, my phone, things I took for granted.

224 | J.D. NETTO

Listening to my sister suffer without any means to help her was the worst pain of all. My muscles and joints hurt, my throat scraped by the cold air.

Maybe this was it.

This was the end.

I closed my eyes as a tear ran down my cheek.

A warm sensation crawled up from my toes to my legs, spreading throughout my body.

My eyes shot open.

I was in a meadow, surrounded by a green forest, the sun high in the blue sky. Blue-feathered birds flew over me, the fluttering of the wings leaving behind a trail of glistening dust. Fear tried to grip me when I realized Ava wasn't at my side.

"You don't need to worry." A deep voice traveled across the atmosphere. "She's safe."

One of the trees uprooted itself from the ground. Branches twirled upward, forming the shape of a man. Leaves joined in a dance, whirling in the air, wrapping themselves into a crown with two antlers. Though there was resemblance of a face, he didn't have any facial features.

"Who are you?" I asked.

"Who do you think I am?" His crown glowed at the echo of his deep voice.

I scratched the back of my head. "Kurah, but shouldn't you look like an elk?" I asked.

"I can take on any shape I like," he replied. "To some I'm an elk, to others I'm what you see."

"Where am I?" I asked.

"You're in your conscience," he replied.

"So I'm still in the cave?"

"Yes and no. You're dying and your spirit is almost leaving your body, so you're in two places at once."

I waited for fear and despair to find me at the sound of his words, but my heart didn't skip a single beat. His presence brought me peace and comfort.

"Is Ava dying, too?" I asked.

"We can talk about Ava later." The branches and roots forming his feet slithered outward, bringing his body closer to me.

"What do you want from me?"

"Maybe I should be the one asking you that question." A breeze sent the trees around me to a dance. "You've always desired another life. You've often called your gifts a curse. Henderbell isn't home, even if you're a Henderbellian by blood. You feel out of place in Albernaith as well. So I'm here to give you what you want. You can leave it all behind and go to a world where you'd never feel pain or sorrow again—a world where you'd belong forever."

"Where's this place you're talking about?" My eyes widened with curiosity.

"My world, beyond the reach of any evil." Branches turned to skin, roots to garments as the crown melted around his head. Before me was a man, skin like a tawny-colored diamond, eyes black like the midnight sky. Resting over his head and draping down his shoulder were the pelts of an elk, the animal's antlers standing above his head. Wisps of his silver hair covered parts of his face, falling down his neck.

"You're nearing death. You and your sister," he said. The texture of the gray garments covering his body resembled reptilian scales.

"Then why isn't she here?" I asked.

"You can choose to leave it all behind," Kurah continued, ignoring my question. "In my world, all the creatures you dreamt of, all the stories you created, all the things you drew in your notebook exist." He smirked.

"How do you know about my notebook?" I asked, cringing at the memory of its destruction.

"I know many things." A smile. "There, you'd forget your parents, Henderbell, those you so despise in school. It would all be erased."

"And you can lead me there now?"

Kurah put his hands together in the shape of a triangle. A flash of light shone from his palms, darting above my head. It dispersed into pieces, moving in the air like fireflies, creating the shape of a doorway.

Kurah strolled to my side, hands folded in front of his body. On his middle finger was an iron ring shaped like two wings "All you have to do is walk through this door."

"That's it?"

"Yes."

I contemplated life without my past. I wanted to forget the fights, the family feud, and the times being different cost me my sanity. Though Henderbell had proven the existence of magic, forgetting it and the nightmare it led me into wasn't a bad idea.

"But," he continued. "You can choose to go back to the cave with your dying sister and fight for Henderbell, your family, and Christmas."

"Christmas?" I scoffed. "Christmas has brought nothing but bad memories in the past few years. Since you know so much, you probably have a vague idea of how many times I wished my family would be mended by coming together on Christmas. I often thought, *'No, this year, it'll be different. We'll all be together and they'll work out their differences.'* But my reality was waking up to my mother screaming or my father breaking a bottle on a wall. I remember the time my grandparents actually arranged to come over for the holidays but all we got that Christmas morning was a phone call."

"I won't blame you if you decide to abandon what you know. But there's great reward for those who turn their brokenness into something beautiful."

"A part of me wants everything to disappear," I confessed. "Christmas. Henderbell. All of it. Honestly, I wouldn't mind forgetting everything."

"You can choose to walk away." The doorway glistened at his voice. "It's your choice."

My whole life flashed before my eyes. The good and the bad. I wanted to gather my memories, split them, toss them in a bag and weigh them on a scale. I glanced at the portal and at Kurah. But Ava's face flashed in my head, her innocent heart, her willingness to believe without question or hesitation. One step could rid me of all my problems, while another would make me face all of them head on.

"They need me," I whispered, hands clenched into trembling fists. "I can't leave them."

"Of course you can." My eyes locked with his. "You can leave them now. You wouldn't be here if you couldn't."

"But I don't want to." My gaze shied away from him.

He chuckled. "I knew I wasn't wrong about you, and I know how much you want to come."

"I do." My chin trembled. "So much."

"One day, you'll leave Henderbell and Albernaith behind to join me in the Everlasting." His garments shifted into roots. "But for now, remember this, you're a prince, crowned with power. Let it be in Henderbell as it is in your heart."

"Are you going to leave me?" I asked.

"I never left." His pelts shifted into leaves. "You just didn't believe enough to see. And there's a reason Ava wasn't here."

"What's that?" I asked.

"She decided to go back to you even before I finished speaking."

A jolt of adrenaline spread down my body. "Of course she did."

"When you go back to the cave, follow the darkness. Don't let fear find you."

Shadows crept around me, hiding the beauty of the forest and Kurah.

# CHAPTER 20

I gasped for air. My throat stung as the cold air shot down my lungs. The cave was dark, my surroundings barely visible.

Ava was beside me, head on my chest.

I curled my numbing toes and stretched my fingers, cringing at the pain.

"Ava." I tapped her shoulder. "Wake up."

She remained immobile as I shuffled in place.

"Ava!" I knelt on the ground, her body in my grasp. "Ava?" My voice, though stuck in my throat, faintly echoed throughout the cave.

Silence.

"No, no, Ava," I croaked.

"Enzo?" she mumbled, fluttering her eyes open as if waking up from a daze.

I let out a sharp breath. "Thought you were dead."

Though visibility was dim, I spotted a trembling smile on her face. "I'm glad you didn't go with him."

"I wouldn't leave you," I said. "But we can talk about this later. We have to go." I got on my feet with trembling knees, and extended my hand to her. Every movement felt like being stabbed in every single one of my joints.

"Where are we going?" she asked while I pulled her up.

"Kurah told me to go deeper into the darkness."

"But we don't know what's at the end. We can't even see anything."

"It might be an unfair thing for me to say, but can you believe me?"

"Of course." She nodded in agreement.

I stretched out my arm, touching the wall of the cave. With slow steps, we ventured into the unseen. The faint sight of the entrance behind me grew smaller, becoming a small dot in the distance. The sound of our chattering teeth joined our footsteps.

I narrowed my eyes, trying to catch a glimpse of what was ahead. A glowing blue circle pierced the darkness. It exploded into thousands of ascending sparkles, which joined together once reaching the roof of the cave, forming countless crooked lines that resembled a lightning storm. Warmth filled our surroundings as they stretched beyond sight, revealing the ruins of an old temple.

Broken statues depicting knights and amazons crowded the ground. There was a set of stairs leading to a platform with a stone well. Above it a strange sight: a bronze bell supported by a piece of wood upheld by two metal bars stuck to the ground. Rows of pillars towered to the roof of the cave, depictions of men and women at war carved on their surfaces.

Ava and I walked up the stone platform. The faint sound of rushing waters crawled into my ears once I stood by the well, its brim covered in some sort of glistening moss. The bell stood an arm's length above my head, rust defacing its surface. Beside it was a thick beige rope, its tip coiled on the ground.

"Do you think we're safe here?" Ava surveyed the well and then shifted her gaze to the streaks of light above us.

"Who knows?" I sighed. "At least it's warm."

"Think the Shadow Spirits are still after us?"

"I think we lost them this time," I answered, struggling to hide the actual answer haunting my mind.

"Maybe we could sleep here," she suggested.

"I think it's a good idea," I said as her eyes shifted to the narrow tunnel stretching behind the well.

"Where do you think that leads?" She fiddled her fingers, biting the corner of her lips.

"We'll worry about that after we get some sleep," I said.

We sat on the ground and reclined our backs against the well. I observed the streaks of light until losing the battle against my eyelids.

"Enzo!" Ava's blaring voice startled me out of my sleep. I jumped up, eyes wide, heart in a race. The ground trembled. The streaks of light slowly receded, the darkness returning. A bellowing roar blared across the cave, one I knew well by now.

"It found us!" Ava screamed. "Enzo, it found us!"

We jumped to our feet. The trembling intensified, the clapper of the bell now moving, striking its bronze surface, composing a haunting melody.

"Do you see it?" I scanned the rocky formations, but there was nothing.

"No, no!" Ava said. "What do we do? Where do we go?"

"We follow the darkness, right?" I looked at the well and back at Ava. "Maybe that's what Kurah meant?"

"What? Jumping inside? That's crazy!"

The chiming of the bell grew louder.

"What part of this has been sane, Ava?" I climbed to stand on the edge of the well, holding on to the metal bar to my right. "Grab my hand!" I shouted.

"We're really jumping?" she said as I pulled her to stand on the edge. "Enzo, you know I can't swim. What if there really is a river down there?"

Another roar echoed. The remaining stripes of light disappeared.

Darkness settled.

"It's either that or being kidnapped by one of them." I squeezed her hand. "Are you ready?"

"Of course I'm not ready!" Her voice joined the growl of the unseen creature.

I pulled her by the wrist once my feet abandoned the edge of the well. The screeches and the chiming continued while my stomach rose to my throat.

The temperature dropped as we plunged. My cheeks flapped while I gained speed, fear a present nightmare.

I managed to look down, catching sight of a glowing gray mist. Once my body pierced it, the darkness was exchanged by a bright light. Mountains were on full display on the horizon, the sun peaking behind them. And below me was a river.

I took in a deep breath.

We plunged into the cold water.

Ava escaped my grasp. I kept my eyes open, watching the current take her away as despair ensnared me. I thrashed my hands and feet, swimming to the surface.

"Ava!" I managed to shout before being pulled under again.

The water was so clear, the bottom of the river was in full view as I was tossed around. I managed to grab the root of a tree sticking out of the rock barrier, pulling myself back to the surface.

"Ava!" I spat out water.

"Enzo, over here!" Ava screamed.

I searched left and right, trying to spot her as the current tried to take me again.

"Ava!" My throat stung. "Where are you?"

"Enzo!" She clung to a rock in the middle of the river. "Help me! Please help…"

The world came to a standstill. I spotted it above me, crawling like an insect, one of the Shadow Spirits.

"Stay there. I'm coming." I jumped back in the water, hoping to find a way to catch her.

The current pulled me under and revealed a hidden nightmare. Another Shadow Spirit lurked beneath the water as I fought my way back to the surface. The creature swam toward Ava, wobbling its body like an eel.

One my sleeves got caught on a tree trunk submerged under the water, its upper half rising to the surface. I latched on to a branch and ripped it away.

I used the trunk to climb my way out the water, relieved to see the tree was close to shore. But fear struck me again. Ava's terrifying screams joined the thundering sound of the current. A Shadow Spirit held her while crawling up the rock formation beside the river.

I let go of the tree, and fought against the current until reaching the shore. I dragged myself out of the water onto the snow, coughing while struggling to breathe. The cold air on my skin felt like blades stabbing my body. The tips of my fingers were blue, my breath smoke. Ahead of me was nothing but trees and ice.

A pain-filled scream echoed. It was Ava.

"No, no, no," I mumbled, rising to my feet, muscles aching.

Another scream.

"Ava!" The taste of blood spread in my mouth. "Ava!"

A loud explosion resounded. Smoke billowed from the forest, spreading in the air. I followed the sight, jumping over rock and branch until spotting Ava standing beside an elf. His silver hair was tied into a tail, a scowl on his face. His purple eyes shifted to me.

"Enzo!" She ran and threw her arms around me.

"I thought you were gone." I squeezed her, body trembling.

"I was so scared," she said behind whimpers, a cut on her right cheek.

"Your lips are purple." I cupped her face between my hands. "We need to find somewhere warm or we're going to die."

"She was lucky I was here," said the elf, a dagger in hand. I recognized the Henderbellian symbol on his armor; cuts and bruises covered his pale face.

"Who are you?" I asked, alarmed. "And what happened to those things?"

"My name is Loomstak." He sheathed the dagger back into the scabbard on his waist. "And those *things* were just killed." He stretched his hand toward us, releasing a sphere of light. It hovered in mid-air, flickering like a flame. "Don't touch it. It's hot."

I stretched my hand in its direction, warmth striking my skin immediately. Ava followed my act. Cracks spread over the surface of his armor, the gash on his cheek stretching from his eyebrow down to his chin.

"I know who you are," Ava said behind chattering teeth. "Ishmael spoke of you."

"You know him?" he asked in a tone of surprise. His neck spasmed left, his tongue bulging under his lower lip.

"*We* do," I added.

Loomstak frowned. "You're Bane's kids, aren't you?"

"Yes," I replied, the sound of the river distant.

"You knew our dad?" Ava asked, water dripping from her hair down to her shoulder.

"I did. And your mother," He added, and stepped closer. "Any news of your grandparents?"

"No," Ava answered. "We saw them being taken by the Shadow Spirits, but nothing after."

"You were lucky I was close. If you weren't taken by them, then the cold alone would've killed you."

"How did you kill it?" I asked. "Doopar killed a Soul Drainer in the castle. I've been curious since."

Loomstak revealed the dagger on his waist. "Blade is made of Sacred Tears. The only metal that can actually kill Shadow Spirits and Soul Drainers. Forget blood magic and all other sorcery used to contain them." His hands fidgeted as his neck twitched right.

"What happened to you and your men?" I observed his fidgeting movements.

"My men and I were near the prison when it ensnared me with its dark magic and made me its host. None of us expected to come across Soul Drainers." Tears welled in his purple eyes. "I could see and feel everything, though I no longer had control over my body. I watched all my men be mutilated and killed while I was spared."

"I'm sorry to hear that," I said.

"How did you escape?" Ava asked, chin chattering.

His body jerked as if struck by a bolt of lightning. He pressed his eyes shut, took in a long breath and said, "I didn't."

I pulled Ava by her arm. "Ava!"

Loomstak's head twitched to the left. He extended his hand toward me, a mist escaping his palm.

Everything disappeared.

# CHAPTER 21

I was inside a barred cell, wrists chained above my head. Torches flickered on the stone walls. The place smelled like mold and rotten eggs. Ava was beside me, also chained at her wrists. Our clothes had been exchanged for dark tattered cloaks.

"Ava." I nudged her with my foot. "Are you alright?"

"Enzo…" she mumbled, opening her eyes, head resting on her shoulder.

"Wake up."

She squirmed once consciousness found her, trying to jerk her wrists free. Her feeble attempts stopped as she scanned our surroundings. "Where are we?" she asked, fear stamped on her face.

"You shouldn't be here." The familiar voice sent my heart to a race, its sound triggering hope and despair. He was under one of the torches, hair tangled, beard stained with mud, body also covered in a dark cloak.

"Grandpa!" My voice boomed, relieved to see he still lived. Seeing him here with me was like being aboard a ship in a storm. No matter the fate the thrashing waves brought with them, we were all to tread the violent waters together.

"You're alive!" Ava's voice broke at the sound of her words.

"And he isn't alone," said Ishmael from the other side, Doopar beside him, wrists and ankles chained. They sat on the ground, dressed in garments similar to ours.

"You're all here." A shaky laugh burst out of me. "You're alive."

"For now," Doopar added, her blonde tresses covering half of her face.

"Where are we?" Ava grimaced, shuffling her wrists.

"In the dungeon of the Prison of Krishmar," Grandpa replied.

"Where's Grandma?" I asked with a shudder.

"I haven't seen her since the day they took us." He bowed his head. "I don't know where she is."

His answer was like a blow to my stomach. "Have they done anything to you, Gramps?" His face blurred behind my welling tears. "Are you okay?"

He frowned. "The most damaging thing is what I've done to myself and our family. Whips, chains, and torture are nothing compared to the wound I've inflicted on all of you."

"Why do you sound so defeated?" I grunted at the pain of the shackles scraping my skin. "I've heard so many great stories about you in the last few days. You're the king of Henderbell."

"And yet the Shadow Spirits found your grandma and I in our home in Dorthcester. Neither one of us suspected they had learned how to travel between time and both worlds. I wasn't able to keep my son and his wife here. You and your sister were never told of your truth. How great of a saint and king am I?" He closed his eyes and nodded. "They found us at our most vulnerable. And now Christmas is almost here. Your grandma is gone. Henderbell and Albernaith will be destroyed."

"Don't say that," Ava admonished. "We need to believe together. We can't just abandon—"

"Belief alone does no good, sweetheart." He reclined his head back on the stone wall, the scratches on his neck now in view. "I believed none other than our family knew how to travel between time. I believed by keeping Henderbell away from you two, no evil would find you. I believed in respecting your father's choice to leave only—"

"You had good intensions, Gramps," I interrupted.

"It doesn't matter how good they were. They started a war." His gaze shifted to the roof of the prison. "I've failed my people. I've failed my family. I've failed Henderbell."

"You aren't dead yet," Ava said. "We're still alive. There's still hope."

His eyes turned to her. "Ishmael told me Kurah found you. He told me what he showed you. He also showed me as a king once."

"I never knew that," Ishmael mentioned.

"No one does," he added. "Not even Mary. He showed me riding on a white stallion, my son at my side, both of us armored from head to toe. The twelve sigils of the Henderbellian Kingdoms danced in the air and then bowed to me. I was fifteen when he appeared. What angers me the most is the fact he never bothered to show me how my kingdom would end."

"I refuse to believe that." I stood on the tips of my toes in an effort to relieve my wrists of the pain of the shackles. "I refuse to believe this is the end. We're still breathing. You're still alive. Kurah came to me as well."

Grandpa let out a heavy sigh. "Seems like he's been visiting anyone who's willing to give him a chance." He gave me a broody stare. "I like your enthusiasm, but there are many things you've yet to learn."

"Do you know magic, too, Grandpa?" Ava groaned.

"I do, but unlike elves, the magic of our family needs an object to be wielded," he said.

"And where's this object?" I asked.

"In the castle. It's a necklace with a pendant shaped like an eight-angled star."

"I saw it in Dad's old bedroom." My words earned a frown from him.

"Impossible. That necklace is kept under lock and key in a safe," he said, confused.

"No, it was in my dad's old bedroom. It was silver and it had roots drawn on the surface." His eyes widened. "I'm telling you, I saw it."

"He did see it," Ishmael agreed. "I also saw it in the room."

"Who put it there?" Grandpa asked.

"I assumed you left it on the shelf for some reason," Ishmael suggested.

A vacant stare took Grandpa's eyes.

"Can we use magic if we get it?" Ava asked.

"You two won't be able to use magic until you're sealed in Henderbell," he replied.

"What does that mean?" I asked as a drop of blood ran down my wrist.

"You need to agree to be bound to your magic, which also brings the responsibility of being a Henderbellian ruler.

And if you ever decide to be a king or a queen, you'd be required to carry the same burden your grandma and I carry. And whoever you marry will carry the same weight. But that's a decision you don't have to—"

Approaching footsteps interrupted his words. A man with three horns appeared on the other side of the cell, an X-shaped scar streaked across his chest.

He put his hands on his waist and trailed his tongue over his lips. "Oh, don't let me stop the fun. I don't like to be the center of attention," he said in a tone of sarcasm, unlocking the barred door. Every hair on my body raised at the sight of his gray eyes as he strolled inside the cell, coming toward me. I had seen those eyes in Dorthcester when the shadow appeared by the stairs.

"We need to have a little talk," he said, unlocking the shackles around my wrists.

"Where are—" Words turned to grunts as he grabbed me by the nape of my neck.

"You bastard!" Grandpa shouted. "Leave him alone. I'll kill you. I will *kill* you!"

"Will you?" he said snidely. "I don't think so."

Ava kept on shouting my name as he dragged me out of the cell.

I jerked my head, hoping to break free from his grasp. He thrust me forward, releasing me from his hold. "Hey! Hey!"

He locked the barred door and held both of his hands in the air. "I just want to talk. You're acting like I'm leading you to a slaughterhouse."

I spotted Ava on the other side of the bars, staring with bulging eyes, blood trickling down her wrists.

"Walk," commanded the three-horned man with a finger pointed over my shoulder.

In front of me was a spiral staircase lit by a single torch. I did as he commanded, venturing into the darkness ahead, every step adding to the certainty that I was going to die today. Blood dripped from the wounds on my wrists. I chanced a look over my shoulder and trembled at the flames reflected on his eyes.

The light coming from the burning torch grew dimmer as the darkness thickened, moving like tossing waves on the ocean. The temperature dropped. Rumbles resounded. The darkness parted like a curtain, revealing a wide empty hall with a white marble floor, every wall covered by a fluttering gray mist. Up on the roof was a symbol: a skull crowned with thorns.

The three-horned man hurried his steps, now walking ahead of me. He halted the moment we stood under the symbol on the roof.

"What do you want?" I asked in a shrill voice.

A wide smile took his face. "Right now, I want you to sit." From each of his hands revolved a mist that assumed the shape of two iron chairs. "Please."

"So you first send someone to kidnap me in the woods, make me your prisoner, and then you want to have a conversation?"

He crossed his arms over his chest, giving me a nod of disapproval. "I do apologize for the chaos, but that was the only way to get you to listen."

"Got a name?" I asked, fingers tingling.

"Oh, of course. Manners. My name is Molock, a Specter of Vaneeries."

"Are *you* going to sit?"

He shrugged and scrunched his face, taking a seat and crossing his legs. He beckoned me to do the same with a wave.

I did as he requested.

"What's a Specter?" I asked.

"I assist my king, Vaneeries," he replied. "Specters are assigned a task and a hive of Shadow Spirits. A Specter ensures the Shadow Spirits get the job done, since their conscience isn't as developed as ours."

"So you've got more brain than the rest of them."

He smiled. "That's one way to look at it."

I leaned forward, elbows on my knees. "Let them go," I said. "I'll do whatever you want. Please."

"One game at a time." He chuckled.

"Is that what this is to you? A game?" My fingers laced together, hands trembling.

"Yes, and you're one of the main pieces." He slouched forward, locking his gray dull eyes with my own. "Now, let me be candid. I want to save you and your sister. I don't see why you have to die."

My head jerked back. "Save me and my sister?"

"You two have potential. I can feel your strength. And since you're the older brother, I thought you and I should have a chat. You do care for your sister, don't you?"

I leaned back and narrowed my eyes. "I know your story," I declared. "Doopar told me."

He took in a breath through gritted teeth. "And what did an elf tell you?"

"I heard two tales, one that spoke of your people, the Meoner, crossing the Crystal Sea to lead an attack against Henderbell."

His face grew rigid. "And the other tale?"

"The elves found a scroll written by your king, Vaneeries. It said you discovered a magic so strong you had to flee your country. Some Henderbellian king...I can't remember his name—"

"King Oden," he added.

"Yes, King Oden saw the potential behind your magic and invited you to work with him, only to have you burned at the stake on Christmas."

"That's one way to look at it." Ghosts seemed to have taken over his eyes. "All we wanted was freedom for the Meoner. We were going to return home after we had settled here to bring the rest of us across the Crystal Sea. We left sons, daughters, husbands, and wives behind. Even if the king knew burning us would imprison our souls forever, he did it anyway— even if this world was also promised to *my* people."

Sluggish footsteps resounded around me. From the whirling mist on the wall appeared walking corpses shielded in broken armor, their bodies covered in wounds. They walked upright, like soldiers following their leader. Their ears gave away their identity. Elves.

"You see what we did to the elves?" He stood to his feet. "See how we've perfected them? This is the redemption my master wishes to bring upon all living things after they're dead. We'll use their bodies to host the Soul Drainers. We'll rebuild Henderbell and create one glorious kingdom, expanding its power to Albernaith by giving both worlds a fresh start."

My fingers grasped the seat of the chair. The putrid stench coming from the lacerated bodies brought a sinking feeling to my stomach.

"There's also something else." The elves shuffled at the sound of his words, standing in two separate lines, creating a walkway between them. My body tensed, my heart ensnared by hopelessness. One elf appeared from the mist on the wall, holding my grandmother by her wrist.

"Enzo!" The sound of her screaming my name stole the air from my lungs. "Don't touch him." Her glasses were cracked, partially hidden by the silver hair falling on her face, her body covered in the same dark cloak I was.

Seeing her dragged by living corpses sparked haunting images in my head of what they might have done to her in the past few days.

"Oh, quiet." Molock grimaced. "She's so loud all the time."

"What do you want from me?" I asked, blood boiling in my veins "I'll do anything. But let my family go."

"A fair trade," he said.

The floor beside me parted, its stones piling on top of one another until forming a well.

"Bring her here." Molock tapped on the brim of the well.

The walking elven carcass dragged her to him, her attention on me.

"Well, sit," he demanded once she was within reach.

Grandma did as he commanded. "Enzo, whatever he asks of you, don't do it."

"Why don't we let Enzo decide this one?" A flush of adrenaline rushed through my body as he laid a hand on her shoulder. "He's a grown boy, after all."

She trembled.

"What do you want?" I insisted.

"The object that allows your family to use magic," he said. "You'd be paying a debt long overdue."

"What debt?" I asked.

"My people were supposed to own that object. Such power was supposed to belong to the Meoner, not to the Griffins," he replied. "And now you have the chance to make this right."

"I don't know what you're talking about," I said.

He grasped my Grandma's arm. I took in a quick breath as he leaned her body toward the mouth of the well. "If this is how you're going to play, then this is how it's going to end."

"You weren't supposed to own anything." Grandma faced him, her face red. "You're all delusional."

"I see we're sticking to your version of the story." Molock tightened his grasp around her arm. "And since we don't have time to discuss that, I'll leave it up for Enzo to decide."

"I'm confused," I said.

Of course I wasn't confused. He wanted the necklace I found in my dad's bedroom.

"Well, don't be. They lied to you. They didn't tell you about Henderbell, about your royal blood. I bet they never even mentioned your bloodline's magic. I'm giving you the chance to rectify that. Join us in building this new world. Give us the necklace and your family lives to see this new empire built."

"Don't do it," Grandma mumbled. "Please, listen to me."

"If you do as she says, she dies. Right here. Right now."

"Better an old woman dead than millions ruled by a tyrant," she declared.

"Grandma, please—"

"Don't even think about joining them!" I had never seen that look on her face before. If her eyes were swords, they would've sliced me open. "There's more in store for you than helping this Specter and his master. If I need to die to make that happen, so be it."

"And what about the men that burned my people?" She shuddered as Molock tugged her closer to his face, their noses inches away. "What do you make of them?" His saliva splattered over her cheeks. "You want us to just forget how we were promised a land of our own? We were willing to work with King Oden on building this world, but when he saw who we really were, he turned his back on us and burned us all."

"I'm ready to die," she declared, her face rigid.

"Grandma, please, don't do this. I can help." I darted to my feet. "I can't…"

"It's alright." Her eyes glistened. "It really is. I'd rather die than see my family and my people suffer at the hands of Shadow Spirits, Specters, and Soul Drainers." She looked at Molock. "Can I at least hug my grandson goodbye? Will you show me that mercy?"

"Unlike those before you." He released her from his hold. "Those that burned me and my people, I'll grant you a final wish so the boy can see I extended mercy when none was shown to me."

She stretched out her arms, beckoning me closer with a wave. I ran to her, wrapping her in a tight embrace. She tilted her body to the side and pulled me down the well.

# CHAPTER 22

The stone walls of the well became a blur. She released me as we plunged into the darkness. I spread out my arms, trying to grasp something, but the well seemed to expand the deeper I got.

Streaks of light spread around me like lightning on a stormy night. From the light appeared faces screaming, and crying; their sounds like a knife scraping my ears. I clutched my hands over my chest and crossed my legs as if going down a slide. My back bumped onto a moist smooth surface, causing my body to lie down. I looked down, spotting a narrow passageway illuminated by a bright light.

I pressed my eyes shut, my body lingering in the air before striking something cold. I rolled across a flat surface until banging against something hard. My eyes fluttered open, a groan followed. I was back in the castle, in front of the Bending Shield in the Hall of Rulers. As I stood up, Grandma spewed out of the canvas, graciously landing on her feet.

She threw her arms around me. I squeezed her as a tear rolled down, my head on her shoulder.

"I thought I was going to lose you," I said, gulping a breath.

"But you didn't." She kissed me on my forehead and cupped my cheeks between her hands. "But we have to hurry. We have to send our armies to the prison to rescue the others." Her words were followed by a dry cough, her face burning red.

"Are you okay?"

"Yes." She sniffled after the coughing ceased. "I'm fine."

"Do they think we died?"

"I'm not sure." She cleared her throat. "But one thing I know. Vaneeries and his Shadow Spirits may have learned how to navigate through time, but they haven't learned everything there's to know about our magic."

"The Bending Shield led us to the hideaway in the Forest of Nick when a Soul Drainer was here and now it just led us back to the castle. How?"

"It can be called upon when two Griffins are present, though it requires a lot of energy to summon it," she said. "Molock had me locked away from your grandpa hoping to stop our magic. But all I needed was another Griffin beside that well to call upon it. And there you were. I'm sure, had they known this little trick, they would have never put us together."

She snapped her fingers. She scanned our surroundings after a few seconds of silence. "Where are they?"

"Mandeerun and Ashtolia? They disappeared since the Soul Drainers attacked."

"I know where they are." She held her arms together, making the shape of an X. She stretched out her fingers, creating the shape of antlers. The patterns carved on the golden wooden frame of the Bending Shield slithered around like snakes, until a small compartment was revealed. Two flames burned inside.

She snapped her fingers twice, and at her action, the flames drifted out of the frame. Fire shifted to golden armor, our faces reflected on their surfaces as the sigil of Henderbell appeared on their breastplates. Their faces were in view, taken by surprise.

"My queen!" Ashtolia exclaimed, both bowing their heads, armors glimmering with their movements. "You're safe."

"Go to the dungeons. Call all the Fire Knights. We march out to the Prison of Krishmar as soon as we can," she ordered. "Call Horthur. Tell him I want to see him in the throne room within the hour." She scrunched her face. "I need to get out of these clothes first."

"Right away," Mandeerun replied. "But before," he looked at me, "Forgive us, prince. The Soul Drainer ensnared us in an illusion. We were only released from it after you and your sister were gone from the castle."

"There's no time for this," Grandma scolded. "He's alive. We're all alive, but if we don't hurry, we may not be for long. Christmas is almost here."

Their bodies shifted to flames and exploded into many particles, which hovered into the black canvas and disappeared from sight.

"Who's Horthur?" I asked.

She took in a long breath, hand on her chest. "The general of the human Henderbellian army. Enzo, listen to me, meet me in the throne room in an hour as well. Go freshen up and change. We have much to discuss."

"Did they hurt you?" I asked, noticing her quivering hand.

"That doesn't matter." She placed a finger under my chin. "I'm here. I'm alright. We'll all be alright."

She had dirt smeared on her cheeks, a cut above her eyebrow and another on her upper lip, stretching up her right nostril.

"Alright…" I shrugged, trying to fight away the many torture scenarios my mind created.

She disappeared behind one of the doors, her dark cloak dragging behind her.

I scanned the hall, observing the broken canvases and portraits on the floor, until spotting my father's face. Despite all the struggles and trials I had faced in the last few days, his face was still the nightmare that haunted me the most.

I entered his old room, chest tight as I thought about Ava chained at her wrist. The necklace with the pendant shaped like an eight-pointed star still sat on the bookshelf by the dresser. I grabbed the object and laid on the bed, gazing at the constellations painted on the ceiling. As I tightened my grasp around the pendant, I finally gave in to the despair lingering in my heart.

They were either going to be saved or we were all going to die.

# CHAPTER 23

I took the entrance from the Hall of Rulers, emerging behind the thrones wearing a red jacket I found in Dad's old wardrobe. The shoulders were stitched to the sleeves by dark thick threads. A silver Henderbellian sigil was sown on the back. Under the jacket, around my neck was the necklace.

Whispers echoed across the room, along with my footsteps. Grandma stood at the foot of the stone platform that led up to both thrones, facing a tall armored man. Two guards were at the main entrance, the ticking of the swaying pendulum an echo.

"Enzo." She turned to me, wearing a red long sleeve with armored pads on its shoulder. There was a pin shaped like the Henderbellian sigil on her chest. Her boots were flat, pants tucked inside of them. "This is Horthur, commander of our human army."

"Prince." He banged a fist over his chest. His shoulders were broad, eyes broody and dark. A silver armor covered his body; antlers rose from his helmet, a dark purple cape draped down his back. A sword clung to the belt on his waist.

"Pleasure," I said. "So, any decisions yet, Grams?"

He looked at Grandma, as if asking permission to share information. She nodded, signaling he was allowed to speak.

"Our army and the Fire Soldiers are ready to march at our queen's command. We'll be a distraction to Molock and those with him, so you and the queen can do your part," he said.

"And what are we doing?" I dawdled.

"There's an object that allows our family to use our magic," Grandma said, seemingly worried. "It's a necklace shaped like an eight-pointed star."

"You mean, this one?" I reached into my shirt and revealed the object.

"How did you find it?" A frown formed on her face as she took a step toward me. The image of the stone platform, the two crystal thrones, and the massive white marble statue of Kurah behind her sent shivers down my body.

"It was in Dad's bedroom," I replied.

"How did it end up there?" She grabbed the object. "Your grandfather keeps it locked in a safe in our room. I was worried when I didn't find it just now."

"I don't know how it ended up on that bookshelf, but we have it."

"We have to enter the prison with this necklace so your grandpa and I can unite our magic," she said.

"My queen," Horthur said. "You should refrain from using your magic. You know you're—"

"I'll be alright," she admonished with a scowl.

"Shouldn't you stay here, Grandma? Wouldn't it help if at least one of you was on the throne in case…well…"

"The curse requires both regent rulers to be on the throne. Our fates are not only bound by magic, but also by duty. The Griffin bloodline—your grandpa's family—was entrusted with the secret of time generations ago. I married into it, and it was eventually passed down to me. The secret gave us a lot of power. In order to keep our hearts in check, our family was also cursed." She took in a wheezing breath.

*When worlds collide on Christmastime*
*When all living things at the gap stand*
*To be one and whole again*
*Should the wielders of time not be home*
*Destruction will strike*
*Upon an empty throne*

"Prince Enzo," Horthur started. "We'll do our best to keep the Shadow Spirits and Soul Drainers outside the prison. That should give you all time to find them."

"How are we going to sneak into the castle?" I asked.

"The Bending Shield will take us back through the well," Grandma replied, her gaze shifting to Horthur. "When you see them gathered in front of the prison," she tucked a hand inside her pocket and revealed a necklace with a round red stone, "let me know."

"At once." Horthur grabbed the jewel. "And you're sure this is the magic you have to use, my queen?" There was a tone of concern in his words.

She replied with a nod of consent. "I'll be fine."

"What will that do?" I asked.

Grandma reached under the collar of her long sleeve, revealing the same necklace. "This will glow red once his energy is channeled to me."

"When would you like us to march out?" Horthur asked.

"Right away," she declared. "Use the night to shield you."

"Question." They both looked at me. "How are we actually going to defeat Molock?" I asked.

"Leave that up to your grandfather and me," Grandma replied, revealing a dagger clinging to the belt around her waist. "That's our job."

"When the lord of the Shadow Spirits sends out a Specter," Horthur started. "Their servants are like parasites latched to their leader. If we kill Molock, his servants will follow. Soul Drainers can't exist on their own. They need a master. Even if they aren't killed, they'll be powerless." His attention shifted to Grandma. "We *will* see Christmas in Henderbell."

"Kurah be with you," Grandma said.

He bowed and left the throne room.

"I should've fought harder for you and your sister," Grandma said the moment the two guards shut the massive doors behind him. "I wish Henderbell had been revealed to you differently."

"At least we know of Henderbell now."

A look of disappointment stained her face. "Your father's old clothes fit you perfectly."

"He had a good sense of style back then."

"We had that made for him on his fifteenth birthday." She sighed. "I wonder if he would've stayed here had we been more accepting of Evelyn when they met."

"How did that go?" I asked.

"A story for another time." There was sadness in her words. She looked at the necklace around my neck and said, "It's called the Seeing Star. It's a very rare object."

"Can you tell me more about our magic?"

"Now *that* I can do." She walked up the steps on the stone platform and sat on the throne. She tapped on the armrest of the throne beside her, beckoning me closer.

I observed Kurah's statue as I marched up the platform. It was as if it was carved to intimidate those who gazed at it. The throne was extremely uncomfortable, its armrests cold. My legs dangled a few inches above the floor.

"The story goes that when King Oden crossed the Crystal Sea from Lestee, he brought with him a witch named Elleanor. She was wise and had been appointed to council him. She spoke of a tyrant, Claudius the Fallen, and how he had kept his people under a harsh rule in a land across the ocean. She also told Oden if he defeated the tyrant, he'd conquer a new world, expanding his dominium. Elleanor knew of Oden's thirst for power, and managed to persuade him to sail to an unknown country while keeping a dangerous secret. She was pregnant with his child and heir. He destroyed Claudius with his army, killed his soldiers and executed the tyrant in front of his own people."

Her voice echoed across the room, the soldiers at the entrance as still as statues

"Their first son, Valk, was born a couple of months after Claudius' defeat, not showing any signs of magic in his blood. They had four more children after, Querth, Nora, Kymern, and Torm. To Elleanor's disappointment, all of her four kids were born without magic in their blood. She spent years searching for a solution on her books and maps until she found a jewel inside one of the chests belonging to Oden."

"Did it have a name?" I asked, arms folded over my chest.

"The jewel of Ostrion. She gathered her four children in secret and had each one touch the jewel, revealing the truth about their powers. They did have magic after all, but running in their blood. The jewel helped her teach them how to wield their magic."

"Did she tell King Oden?" I asked.

"She did. He was happy and disappointed," she replied.

"Disappointed?"

"The jewel didn't give *him* any power, or so he thought." She smirked. "There's something called Blood Impartation, which means once one is united with a Griffin in blood, magic is transferred. But she never told him."

"Why do I think Elleanor is a backstabber?" I frowned.

"I wouldn't call her a backstabber. I'd call her a woman with a plan," she answered. "King Oden's rule at the time was strong. He made powerful alliances with the other

Henderbellian kingdoms after defeating Claudius—many happy to be free of a tyrant. But unfortunately, a conqueror's heart is always prone to deceit. Elleanor showed him a world untouched, hidden through a passageway on a tree accessible only by those who could wield time. She poisoned his mind to think his kingdom needed even more expansion. King Oden ordered his sons, Kymern and Torn, to enter this new world, told they could safely return."

"Did they use that tree to go to Albernaith?" I asked.

"They did." Her dry cough whirled across the throne room. "After a week without news," she continued, clearing her throat at her every word. "Elleanor went to the Tree of Hender and opened the portal, finding a small populated village. But in front of her were two graves with her children's names."

"She was too late in time," I said.

"Exactly. She told King Oden what happened. He was consumed with rage and blamed his wife for their deaths. He claimed her dark magic cursed them. She was ordered to live out her life in the highest tower of this castle, locked away with her books and magic. She spent the rest of her days studying a way to navigate time between both worlds.

"King Oden died of an illness, Elleanor followed months later," she continued. "Inside her chambers they found a book she'd written her daughters, Qerth and Nora. In it were not only the secrets to their magic, but she discovered a gap between both realms that allowed time to flow the same for twenty-four hours."

"Is there a way to go back in time?" I asked, hoping for a positive answer

"No, if the portal of the Tree of Hender is opened at a certain moment, that's where time will be. But in the book, she wrote about three major stars aligning on Christmas, their act allowing time to flow the same way in both places. She wrote: *The ability to wield time mirrors an artist's drawing. First there are lines that make a vague sketch. Details are created. Lines are thickened. Color is added. A full picture is painted.*'"

"You memorized all that?" I was surprised.

"I married into the family. I went through the Blood Impartation. I had to learn," she replied.

"When Molock appeared to me at your house as a shadow," I said. "It told me my blood was cursed."

"And it is," she said in flat voice. "King Oden's illness was no accident. Her magical discoveries required a sacrifice."

My eyes widened. "Elleanor killed the king?"

"And with his death, came the curse in your blood," she revealed. "In the book she left her daughters, she explained she had given them the gift of magic, but she'd also given them the gift of a curse. They were also responsible to keep an eye on the world their siblings had created as well. And that's how this responsibility rests on our shoulders, and it'll rest on yours and

Ava's if you say yes to your magic." She laid a hand over mine. "But Elleanor had another child with another king in Lestee before she sailed to Henderbell with Oden."

"What?" My voice took on a higher pitch.

"He was named Vaneeries." Her gaze left me, turning to the pendulum on the wall.

"The king of the Shadow Spirits," I mumbled.

"Vaneeries has a claim to the Seeing Star and once his truth was revealed to him, he spent years gathering the Meoner to strike Henderbell. Elleanor knew she was his mother, but she let Oden burn him and his people after their arrival in Henderbell."

"What if I don't want magic?" My eyes shifted to the swaying pendulum. "What if I never want to have anything to do with it?"

"You can make your choice, just like your father and mother did." A shiver shot down my body. "I know it's unfair to carry this burden. I know you didn't ask for it, unlike me. But truth has been revealed to you. Now you get to decide what to do with it."

# CHAPTER 24

When Grandma woke me up before daybreak, she brought into my room a tray with fruits, bread, and milk. She was still in the same clothes from yesterday, the dark circles around her eyes looking more like bruises, her silver curls falling on her shoulder. I had fallen asleep without a change of clothes, the Seeing Star around my neck.

She left the room without saying a word. What was there to say when you knew you might meet death in a few hours? I ate gazing at the starlit night outside the window and once finished, joined her in the hall.

She stood in front of the Bending Shield, arms crossed in front of her. She had the red jewel in her trembling hand, dangling by its thin metal chain.

"Do you want the Seeing Star?" I asked, sure my heart was going to explode out of my ribcage.

"Keep it." Her attention remained fixed on the dark canvas. "It'll be safer with you."

"So we just stand here and wait until that jewel glows?" My hands sweat cold.

"Yes."

The hovering silence between us inspired my mind to speak. Though I was determined to save them, what was going to happen after? Was I supposed to become king of this place? Would I be rejected like my father was for not saying yes to the magic of my family?

I shuddered once the jewel glowed red.

"Stay close," she whispered, waving her hand in front of the canvas.

As the patterns carved on the wooden frame moved, I glanced around the hall one more time, spotting my father's picture. Anger and resentment turned to curiosity. If I was allowed to keep my life, the first thing I was going to do was ask the real reason he rejected his magic.

Grandma stepped into the Bending Shield.

I followed.

An unseen force pulled me upward. The streaks of light appeared again, along with the suffering faces. Above me was a glare of light, growing wider with my every breath.

I darted out of the stone well like a pebble thrown in the air, falling on my back. Grandma graciously landed on her feet. The stones on the floor flattened, returning to their original form.

The walls covered in a gray mist exploded into ash. A layer of ice spread over the marble floor, shattering into particles that turned to snow. The symbol of the skull crowned with thorns on the roof shattered. The entire structure of the prison vanished. Mountains and trees were now in view, rising in front of the dark sky now tainted with subtle hints of a sunrise. The cold winter air tortured my face as the sound of a blowing horn bellowed in my ears.

"How much of a fool do you think I am?" said a voice behind me. Grandma's head jerked back.

Molock stood with a smug smile, chest bare despite the frigid temperature, the X-shaped scar on his chest in view. My grandfather, Ava, Doopar, and Ishmael knelt in front of him, wrists crossed in front of their bodies as if chained.

"Enzo!" Ava screamed, still wearing the dark cloak. "You're alive. You're okay."

"Shut it, girl." Molock pushed Ava out of his way as he stepped closer.

Behind them was the moat, crowded with elves—or whatever they had become now that the Soul Drainers lived in them. And waiting on the other side were hundreds of

Henderbellian soldiers. There were spheres of light scattered among them, like torches burning in the distance. I could only assume the Fire Knights had marched with them.

"You all fell right into our trap." He halted. "Did you really think I didn't know what would happen if Enzo was with you?" He nodded as if disappointed. "I didn't put you with the king because I needed Enzo and his sister. I knew you were going to play your little trick, Mary. But you failed. Who do you think put the Seeing Star in Bane's old room?"

"It couldn't have been you," she said, the muscles on her face trembling. "You couldn't have entered that castle."

"No, I'm not worthy of such merit." He pressed his lips into a line. "But there might be a traitor in the family."

"Whatever he asks of you." Grandpa glared with eyes that could cut bones. "Don't do it."

"Oh, I think he will." He continued on toward me.

"Stay where you are!" Grandma demanded, a cough following her order.

He sniggered. "You think you can give orders here?"

Another blow of the horn. The Henderbellian army marched through the snow-covered valley, their shouts echoing in the air. Despair shrouded Grandma's face as towering flames scattered over the Henderbellian soldiers. Pain-filled screams drifted like a dark symphony, the smell of burning flesh polluting the air.

Two flames appeared beside Molock, exploding into particles. They joined together, taking the shape of two bodies. I shuddered once their familiar faces were in view.

"No," Grandma moaned. "No, no…"

Mandeerun and Ashtolia smiled.

Footsteps approached behind me. It was Loomstak, or whatever was left of him, one of his purple eyes now a carved hole on his pale face.

Ishmael followed his every move until Loomstak found a place beside Molock.

"Surprised?" Molock smirked.

"Why?" Grandpa asked, chin wobbling. "Just tell me why."

"You'll see why," Ashtolia said. "Don't worry, king. You won't miss a thing this time."

The look on Grandpa's face was like a dagger to a heart.

"I'm sorry you weren't informed that a couple of your servants switched sides," Molock said snidely. "It hurts, doesn't it? When something that belongs to you is taken in secret?"

Grandma's chin trembled, the veins on her neck visible.

"They'll all die in vain." Molock smiled as the army of dead elves darted across the moat, screeching, growling, and roaring. "Burned and devoured." His gray eyes locked into mine. "Have you ever seen war, Enzo? Ever seen a man bleed to death?" He chuckled. "Of course you haven't. Maybe it's time to remediate that."

He waved a hand in the air. For a moment, it was as if the ground had been stolen from beneath my feet. Doopar's body hovered at his movement, drawing closer to him until floating at his side. She grunted and thrashed, trying to break free from whatever magic had her.

"Give me the Seeing Star or she's the first one to go."

Grandma reached for her belt and unsheathed the dagger, thrusting it at Molock. He grabbed the weapon by its hilt in mid-air and tossed it on the ground, the object disappearing amidst the dead. Grandma stretched her arm and opened her hand, revealing a flash of red light, but the sight was replaced with pain-filled groans and coughs. She fumbled back, gasping for air.

I held her by the arm before she fell on the ground.

"That was a sweet gesture, Mary." Molock clicked his tongue. "Rude to toss a blade at me, but still sweet. The elf lady tried the same thing and look how that turned out."

"Whatever he does to me or to your grandfather, don't give him that Seeing Star," Grandma demanded, the muscles on her face twitching.

"Enzo," Molock said. "Look at Doopar. Look at your elven friend."

I did as he requested, pain gripping my chest.

"Ah, there's more than just friendship, isn't there?" Her body drifted closer, her face inches away from mine, her breath touching my cheeks.

Grunts, groans, and the clanging of metal blared from the battle; the smell of burnt flesh pungent. A cloud of smoke billowed into the air, spreading across the sky as the rays of the morning sun pierced the darkness.

"I'll say it one more time," Molock continued. "Give me the Seeing Star and I'll release her."

"Enzo," Doopar's voice was weak. "It's alright."

"No, no, no—"

"Enzo! It's alright."

"Don't say that."

"If the Seeing Star falls in his hands, we're all going to die sooner or later. I'd much rather die knowing I protected Henderbell."

"Please, don't speak as if—"

The sound of bones crunching stabbed my ears. A quivering breath escaped her lips. Her purple eyes bulged out of their sockets. Blood streaked down her nostrils as she released a sigh, her head dropping like a bird shot by a stone.

Ava's screams pierced the atmosphere.

Doopar's body was tossed to the side, rolling on the ground like an empty bottle.

"And I can crush every single heart in this room." Molock guffawed, chest out. "This is all very thrilling. As you can see, I'm patient, but you're getting on my nerves."

"You killed her." I was frozen, trying to find reason again while seething with anger.

Grandma ran to Doopar's body, kneeling beside her.

The moat behind Molock was overrun by running corpses. Blood stained the snow on the valley, where the dead piled up. Columns of fire spread through the fighting armies, torching every Henderbellian soldier, their screams the haunting symphony of the dead. Ishmael grimaced, shuffling in place, trying to break free from whatever force held his hands, his eyes shifting between Doopar and Loomstak. Grandpa wheezed, his deadpan stare on me.

"Who's next?" Molock scanned their faces.

"Stop your whining, Specter," Grandpa said weakly. "Your problem is with me. Why not take me instead?"

"Father Christmas." Molock smiled, arms spread out. "Such bravery. Or maybe a death wish? You have no crowned successor to the throne of Henderbell. Be careful."

"Vaneeries is a coward." Grandpa curled his hands into fists, arms trembling. "He had to send you and your slaves to do his bastard bidding. He couldn't face me or my family. That's what this is about. His claim to my magic. His bitterness toward his mother who watched you all burn like cooked meat."

Molock's face grew rigid.

"Why couldn't he face me alone?" Grandpa continued. "Why do all this? My wife wasn't born into magic. She learned it. It must be a sad thing to serve a coward king who'd much rather hide behind his slaves. You're only his reflection."

"And it must be a sad thing to know your son deserted you." Molock's chest raised with a breath and at the wave of his hand, Grandpa was pulled up to stand on his feet by an unseen force, his hands jolting free.

"No!" I shouted. "Not him. Please not him. No."

Ava stared, jaw wide open, her face pale.

"Is this what you want?" Molock asked. "To die in front of your family?"

"Prove to me you're no coward." Grandpa opened and closed his hands as if trying to relieve them from pain. "Give me a sword and we'll do one-on-one combat? If you win, you can have the Seeing Star."

"Nicholas, don't," Grandma begged, still kneeling beside Doopar, surrounded by a puddle of blood.

"I like that idea." Molock grabbed the sword inside the scabbard on Loomstak's belt, dropping it on the floor. "Take it. The blade is made of Sacred Tears. This thing can send me and the others right back to where we came from. But I promise you, I'll defeat you and avenge my kind and my king."

He grabbed the sword by its hilt.

"Grandpa, can I help?" I asked

"Of course you can." Molock uncurled his fingers and between his palm appeared a glare of light that took on the shape of a sword. Once the light receded, it revealed the weapon's jagged rusty blade. "Give the Seeing Star to your grandmother."

"Enzo, do as he says." Grandpa ordered, eyes fuming.

I froze in place, trying to find an alternative to the request.

"Just do it!" he shouted.

I rushed to Grandma's side while removing the necklace. I placed it on her hand, shuddering at the image of Doopar's dead body. Her hair was strewn across the snow, her face pale, the streaks of blood running down her nostrils covered in ice. Grandma's teary eyes locked with mine. We didn't need words to understand each other. We both knew death could become our closest friend in a few moments.

Loomstak strolled amidst the dead elves surrounding us, and then appeared holding the dagger my grandmother tossed at Molock.

"If any of you try to help him," Molock said. "Loomstak will be the first to plunge a dagger in your hearts."

He swayed his sword at Grandpa, who managed to dodge the blow by holding his blade over his face. Grandpa wheezed, his arm trembled.

"You've got some skill in you still, old man!" Molock strolled around him like a predator and struck again. Grandpa managed to swerve away.

Blades snapped at each other as their feet danced on the floor. Fast were the cuts and slashes from their weapons, but they managed to dodge all of them. Molock curled a hand into a fist and struck Grandpa's face, the blow sending him to the snow-covered ground, the sword slipping from his hand.

Blood streamed down my grandfather's nostrils. While still on the ground, he rolled past his opponent and grabbed his weapon, but once he tried to stand, Molock's knee struck his face, drops of blood jolting into the air, staining the snow.

A cold breeze touched my face as I watched Grandpa squirm. But my true despair was knowing there was nothing I could do to help. Grandma's body fidgeted with every sound from the fight while keeping her eyes on Doopar.

Molock grabbed Grandpa by the nape of his neck, who managed to jerk his head free from his captor's hold.

Blades danced once again.

"So much for saving Christmas, Saint Nicholas," Molock shouted, circling Grandpa with his sword pointed at him.

My lungs failed to draw breath as Loomstak lunged the dagger in his hand into Grandpa's thigh. He screamed, dropping his sword and pressing a hand over the wound flowing with blood.

Grandma abandoned Doopar's body and darted toward Grandpa's direction as Loomstak marched closer to Ava.

Molock's fingers curled into the palm of his hand, as if holding something in his grasp. The tormenting sound of my sister squealing like a dying pig made me certain we were all going to die. She bent her body forward, pressing her forehead on the ground.

"One more step, Mary, and she dies."

"You coward!" Ishmael shouted, saliva splattering out of his mouth. "Coward. Damn you, Molock."

"I said I was going to fight. Never said I was going to play it clean." Molock wiped his lips with a wrist.

Ava cringed and then gasped for breath.

Molock ensnared Grandpa by the hair, lifting his head.

"Look at them." Molock ordered. "Look at them and tell them you failed."

Grandpa's gaze remained on the ground.

"Look at them." Molock's voice was deeper. He pulled his head up, forcing him to lift his eyes. "Tell them how you failed."

Silence.

"Tell them! Tell them! Tell…"

Molock's words faded into silence as I watched the unimaginable. Ava jumped to her feet, her wrists jolting to the side of her body as if breaking away from her invisible chains. In the blink of an eye, she grabbed the dagger from Loomstak's hand and ran to Molock, who had his back toward her. The dark cloak covering her body flowed behind her like the smoke rising from the burnt corpses in the valley. I had never seen her eyes consumed with so much rage. Her feet abandoned the ground as she raised the blade in the air. Before Molock had a chance to turn, the dagger plunged into the nape of his neck. Ava fell to her side, quickly crawling away from him.

He released Grandpa and reached for the blade, his eyes jumping out of their sockets. With fumbling hands, he turned around, searching for the culprit. A dark liquid rushed out his nostrils like a river. He fell to his knees, his gaze on Ava. He opened his mouth to speak, but before he uttered a single word, his body burst into ashes and drifted away.

Ashtolia and Mandeerun shifted into flames and hovered away. In the distance, the Fire Knights jolted upward, crowding the dawn tainted by a smoke cloud with flickering balls of fire. Beyond the moat, the dead elves exploded into ashes. The snow under my feet was replaced by marble. A mist appeared around us, moving in circles like a tornado. The walls were once again visible, the mountains and trees no longer in sight. The sigil of the skull crowned in thorns was above me, and the structure of the prison appeared as if it had never vanished.

I rushed to Ava, who stared without a single movement, face pale.

"Hey." I shook her shoulders while gasping for air. "Are you alright? You okay?"

She replied with vacant eyes, jaw open.

"Ava," I insisted. "Can you hear me?"

She remained as still as a statue, staring at the same spot where Molock knelt before he disappeared.

Ishmael rushed to Loomstak as he fell forward, managing to catch him before he struck the ground.

"You're alright," he said, tears streaming down his face. He sat on the floor and laid Loomstak's head on his lap. "We're going to get out of here. I promise everything will be alright."

Surprise took Ishmael's face after Loomstak managed to smile.

"Are you still in there?" Ishmael asked, voice caught in his throat.

"Yes and no." Loomstak winced, body trembling. "The Soul Drainer is still inside of me and it's fighting to stay." A scream burst out of him, the veins on his neck bulging under his skin. "I keep fighting it away so I can at least say goodbye…"

"Don't say that." Ishmael clutched Loomstak's hand, his tears dripping on his face. "You'll be alright. You'll see."

"I don't blame you." Loomstak groaned. "You were being a faithful servant." Ishmael pressed his forehead against Loomstak's, their noses touching. "I tried to do as you wanted. Sorry I..." His skin turned to dust and his clothes to ash.

Ishmael screamed, banging his fists on the marble floor.

Grandma was beside Grandpa, his head on her lap, the Seeing Star now in his hand. She caressed his face, a sad smile on her lips.

"Go to him," Grandpa whispered, his hand on her cheek. "Ishmael needs you more than me."

She gave him a kiss on the forehead and gently laid his head on the floor. She walked to Ishmael and wrapped him in her arms. He buried his face in her neck, his sobs a loud echo.

"Enzo," Ava whispered, eyes still haunted. "I killed him."

"You did," I said with a shudder. "You were very brave."

"But I killed him."

"You still saved us."

"But *I* killed him."

Her eyes burned with rage—something I had never seen before.

"He was our enemy, Ava." I cupped her face in my hands. "He was evil."

She slowly gave me a nod of disagreement, lips pressed together. "There's no good or evil. Just perspective."

My eyes shifted to Doopar's body. She had spoken those exact words moments after she found us in the forest.

"Go to her," Ava whispered. "Go see her."

My brows pulled into a frown. A puddle of blood had formed around Doopar's head. Her back was toward me, her fair hair strewn on the floor.

"Go," Ava insisted.

"You're okay?" I asked.

"I'm alive," she answered.

I got on my feet and walked toward Doopar. Every muscle in my body trembled, but it was the sight of her empty purple eyes that triggered my tears. Her face was the most beautiful thing I had ever seen. And now here she was. Lifeless. Dead. Gone.

"Thank you." I knelt beside her and stroked her cold cheek. "For everything."

A part of me expected her to answer, but of course that wasn't going to happen.

I scanned her face one more time and turned to Grandpa. He held the Seeing Star over the wound on his leg, the jewel wrapped in light. In seconds, the gash and blood disappeared.

"You have a lot to learn," he said, probably noticing the confused look on my face.

He stood to his feet and walked to Ava, wrapping her in his arms.

"You did a great thing," he said, lips close to her ear. "You were so brave."

"I'm glad you're okay," Ava mumbled.

"How did you do that?" His brows pulled together. "How did you break free from Molock's magic?"

She replied with a shrug and a deadpan face.

With a kiss on her cheek, he released her and approached Ishmael and Grandma, both still kneeling on the ground.

"Ishmael." Ishmael's eyes followed his voice. "I know you're hurting. I know you're in pain, but I need to ask one more thing from you."

Ishmael wiped the streaks from his cheeks. "Yes?"

"Take Mary and Ava to the castle." A portion of the marble on the floor moved, stacking up until forming the round shape of the well. "I'm letting you go through the Bending Shield. Mary is too weak. She can't go alone."

"Aren't we going with them?" I asked, leaving Doopar's body, walking toward them.

"Not yet," he answered.

"What about Doopar's body?" Ishmael's question was met with a scowl from Grandpa.

"Bring her with you," he replied in a cold voice.

Ava walked to stand in front of Ishmael.

"Thank you," she said.

A shudder escaped from him. "You're thanking me?" He wagged his head with flaring nostrils. "Thank *you*, princess, for saving all of us."

Grandma's coughs blared across the room. She cleared her throat, taking in a long breath.

"We better go," Ishmael said, eyes still glimmering.

Ava turned to me. "I'll see you soon."

Ishmael carefully picked up Doopar's lifeless body from the ground, her fair hair stained with blood. I still expected her to move, to breathe, but she remained still. He jumped inside the well. Ava and Grandma followed. The ground flattened as soon as they were out of sight.

"Is there anything you'd like to tell me about your sister?" he asked.

"What do you mean?" Our eyes locked.

"She's never been around magic until arriving in Henderbell?" Wrinkles appeared on his forehead.

"No," I answered, confused.

"You're sure?"

I opened my mouth to affirm I was sure she'd never seen magic before. But I couldn't. The truth was, I didn't know. I didn't understand magic enough to make such an affirmation.

"Follow me," Grandpa said after my brief silence, waving his hand in the air as if conducting a choir. The gray mist covering the wall in front of us parted, revealing the moat.

Once we stepped through the passageway between the mist, it closed like a curtain. Behind me was now the stone structure of the prison, its square-shaped architecture, the tower once again in the middle, the symbol of the crowned skull on its surface.

We walked across the moat, the billowing cloud of smoke rising from the valley our destination. The smell of burnt flesh grew more pungent with my every step. The piles of burning corpses became clearer as we got closer, the moans and screams of the survivors louder.

Hoof beats approached as we neared the valley. Horthur emerged from the smoke wall. His horse neighed at our sight, its coat releasing glowing particles that resembled fireflies. Blood was smeared on his face. The antlers that once rose from his helmet had been reduced to stubs, the surface of his silver armor scratched.

"My king." Horthur bowed his head.

"Thank you for everything," Grandpa said in a quivering voice.

"We did nothing but fulfill our duty," he replied.

"And Ghenthar?" Grandpa asked.

"Unscathed," he answered. "Citizens are preparing for Christmas. There were rumors of your disappearance, but many thought it to be nothing but random talk. We managed to keep everything concealed."

Even trying my hardest, my attention remained on the dead bodies behind Horthur. Many of them were torched, their remains nothing but burnt flesh clinging to bones. The soldiers who had lived walked among the corpses like ghosts. Of one thing I was absolutely certain; their faces were going to haunt my dreams for a long time.

"Before you go back, say your prayers and burn the rest of the dead," Grandpa said, his posture rigid.

Horthur nodded in agreement, pulled the reigns of his horse and returned to the piles of the dead.

Grandpa's eyes glistened as we walked back to the prison. The cloud of smoke crawled above us, covering a portion of the sky as though dawn hadn't come yet. Ashes fell like snow, piling on our shoulders, latching on to the tattered surface of his dark cloak and my scarlet coat.

"Be strong for those looking for strength." His voice broke at the sound of every word. "But don't forget to comfort your own soul." His eyes locked with mine, apparently having the ability to stare into my very soul. "Remember this if you ever decide to claim your magic and crown."

"I will," I mumbled.

"Wisdom is the magic all living things should pursue," he said. "I hope you seek it in the days to come."

# CHAPTER 25

It was Christmas morning. Ava and I were told to meet our grandparents in the throne room before breakfast. I picked a dark red velvet shirt from Dad's old wardrobe. It had a laced collar, the swirls on the fabric stitched with black thread. While getting dressed, my mind replayed the images of Ava grabbing that dagger and plunging its blade into Molock's body. Grandpa's question about witnessing magic before Henderbell spiked even more confusion. Were there any signs before? Did I miss them?

After I was fully dressed, I spotted my old clothes folded inside the wardrobe. Though it had been less than a week since we left Dorthcester, seeing them was a reminder that I was never going to be the same again.

Then I remembered I had left the piece of parchment paper with the word 'Henderbell' inside one of my pockets. I retrieved it and stared at the ornamental letters for a while. I put my old clothes back in the wardrobe and then put the parchment in my pocket.

I closed the wardrobe and glanced at the fresh wounds on my wrists, the image of Doopar's lifeless face overtaking all other thoughts. I feared I was never going to be able to remember the beauty of her face, only the ghost that stole it.

The light of the morning sun shone through the tall stained-glass window as I walked down the Hall of Rulers, casting a spectacle of colors around me. I observed every canvas, both broken and whole, the faces of the men and women in my family—my real family. Conquerors, kings, and queens who had achieved greatness in this world.

I opened the door leading into the throne room, its creaking sound triggering flashbacks of the Soul Drainer attack. The magic and the nightmare of the past few days was going to stay with me for a long time.

The throne room was empty, the pendulum still, pointing downward. I glanced up at both thrones on their platform of stone, my attention shifting to Kurah's statue behind them. I walked up its steps, and stood before them. My hand reached for the arm of the throne to my left, touching its cold surface. I observed the antler rising from the back, conflicted, weighing the blessing and the curse that followed my decision to not only embrace magic, but to be the prince of Henderbell.

"Even if we don't want it..." Ava's voice pierced the silence. She stood at the foot of the platform, wearing a silver dress that parted around her waist, revealing her dark pants tucked into her brown boots. "Even if we say no, we still carry magic."

I hadn't seen her since yesterday. I searched for words of wisdom I could give her, but the image of her face and the memory of the rage that consumed her eyes when she stabbed our enemy didn't allow me to find any.

"Are you scared of our magic?" She walked up the steps.

"After what I saw yesterday, I'm not sure if it's fear or doubt," I replied. "Do you want it? The magic? The power?"

"I do," she replied before I could take a breath, eyes shimmering.

"Even after what you did in that prison yesterday?" I sat on the throne to my left. She sat on the other.

"It's part of being a queen. I know when I'm one, I'll do what I can to stop things like that from happening again. And it's not like I killed a human. My perspective is that I did what I needed to save you."

"And your conscience isn't heavy about what you did?" I shrugged. "I mean, taking a life…"

"I won't allow it to be," she said without any remorse.

"I guess I need to find the same confidence you have," I mentioned.

"You decided to stay, even when Kurah gave you the option to leave it all behind, Enzo," she said. "You were very brave."

"Doopar still died. All those Henderbellian soldiers and those elves and Loomstak..."

"I guess bravery isn't the recipe to save people from death."

"I guess not."

"But when we rule, we can change so many things for the better. You'll see."

*When we rule.* She was so sure I wanted this. I had always wanted magic, but I'd never wanted to be king of anything.

Approaching footsteps echoed. My grandparents emerged, dressed in the most beautiful garments. A scarlet cape draped behind Grandpa, over his shoulder were metal pads with antlers rising from them. Grandma's dress was blood red, with golden patterns sown on the fabric. Their silver crowns resembled branches twisted in the shape of antlers.

Grandpa approached us with a smile. "You seem to be enjoying yourselves."

Grandma followed him, walking at a slower pace taking in long breaths.

"We owe you an apology," Grandpa said once Grandma caught up with him, standing in front of us. "We never desired for you to discover Henderbell and your story like this."

"It's alright." Ava jumped to her feet and slapped her hands on her thighs. "We're still here. You're still here. We're all alive."

"Thanks to you," Grandpa said.

"Your bravery will inspire many," Grandma added.

"There's so much you need to know, so many things you need to learn." Grandpa removed the Seeing Star from under his black shirt, holding it in his hand. "This belongs to you as much as it belongs to me. You're my blood and I promise to pass on the wisdom of this magic, if you ever want it."

"Thank you," I said, shuffling on the throne. "Can I take my time to think it over?"

From the corner of my eye, I spotted Ava's look of disbelief at my answer.

"Of course," he replied. "You can also still think about living with us in Dorthcester."

I chuckled. "That offer is still standing?"

"Of course," he said.

"Can we live here instead?" Ava asked with excitement in her voice.

"All in due time, sweetheart." Grandma coughed.

"Are you sure you're okay?" I asked.

"I'll be for today." She smiled.

"Every Christmas morning," Grandpa started. "The king and queen of Henderbell must be on the throne so prosperity may find both Henderbellians and Albernaithians. If you don't mind, your grandma and I need to take a seat."

"Oh, of course." I jumped to my feet.

"But before we do what we have to do," he continued as they sat on their thrones. "I wanted to show you something." He held out the Seeing Star. "I want you both to touch it."

Ava jolted her hand forward, grabbing the object, a broad smile on her face.

I stared at the necklace. Though reluctant, I did as he requested. A glare of light shone from it, engulfing our hands. It billowed upward like smoke, spreading above us, assuming the colors of the rainbow. The sight exploded into glimmering dust, disappearing before touching the ground.

"What was that?" I took a step back, a grin on my face, my pulse pounding in my ear.

"That was incredible!" Ava said with a clap.

"That was your Christmas gift." Grandpa laughed, clearly noticing the surprise on our faces. "A taste of the magic in you."

"I want more," Ava said.

"Be patient," Grandma said. "All good things come to those who wait."

They held each other's hands. Light wrapped the antlers rising from each throne and expanded across the room, engulfing the pendulum. It took on the shape of an illuminated elk and like a ghost, darted through one of the stained-glass windows. Music echoed in the air. Laughter followed. The sound of fireworks and drums joined in an unusual symphony. They seemed to be coming from outside the walls of the castle.

Ava opened one of the windows. The sight made my knees tremble. Just like the moon is seen before the sun sets, Earth was displayed in the sky. Only it was much bigger than any moon I had ever seen. Every street was overrun with people jumping and dancing. Fireworks of many colors painted the sky.

The doors of the throne room opened. Ishmael entered, dressed in purple, the pin on his chest shaped like Henderbellian sigil. His hair was tied into a bun, hands folded over his body. His eyes red, cheeks puffed.

"They're ready for you both," he said, but even his smile wasn't enough to hide his sorrow.

Grandpa and Grandma walked down the platform and approached him.

"I know you're in mourning." Grandpa held one of his hands. "But it was because of an elf that we survived. It was because of an elf that my grandchildren came to you. They didn't die in vain, and they'll be remembered by all their great sacrifices."

"Thank you," Ishmael said, holding back his tears.

"Where are we going?" Ava asked.

"I promised you were going to see Christmas in Henderbell." Ishmael sniffled. "This is me keeping my promise."

We followed him out of the throne room to a golden double door. Their surface was smooth, the Henderbellian sigil carved at the center of each door. They parted, revealing a set of spiraling stairs that led us up to a door made of wood. Grandpa held Grandma's hand.

"I thought I wasn't going to live to see this day," she said, the corner of her lips curving into a smile.

"But here we are," Grandpa added, opening the door.

Before us was a balcony facing Ghenthar, in sight a multitude of people. Grandpa and Grandma stepped forward. The cheers grew louder, the music happier, the sky completely crowded in fireworks. They looked at Ava and I with a smirk, waving us to stand beside them. The ocean of people stretched as far as I could see, mountain ranges covered in snow surrounded the entire city.

"Henderbellians." Grandpa's voice echoed louder than the screams. I noticed his hand wrapped around the Seeing Star.

"Once again we gather to celebrate Christmas and the hope that's still alive in our midst."

They cheered even louder.

"On this Christmas day." Grandma's voice also drowned the noise coming from the city. "We also celebrate mercy and those who fight for our freedom in the shadows."

"Celebrate truth," Grandpa shouted, the crowd shouting the same back.

"Celebrate courage," Grandma's voice boomed, the people shouted the same.

"Celebrate Henderbell," Grandpa and Grandma's voices carried out together.

Magic was real even when I didn't know it existed. And now I could never deny it. Here I was, standing before my people, surrounded by my blood, with magic running through my veins. Maybe this was the reason why I had always felt like an outsider growing up. I never belonged in the ordinary. I was born to live amidst magic.

# CHAPTER 26

After lunch, my grandparents said they had a surprise for Ava and me in the forest. It was strange to see them riding horses, and since none of us knew how to do the same, we had to hold on to them the whole way.

As we rode through the woods, the blue of the sky was replaced by gray clouds. A light snowfall followed. I suspected where we were going. A few moments later, my suspicion was confirmed. The Tree of Hender was in front of us, its twisted branches covered in snow.

"Why are we here?" Ava asked, hands on Grandpa's waist.

"We're going home," he replied in a tone of excitement.

"No," Ava protested. "I want to stay. I don't want to go back home. How can I live there now that I've seen all of this?"

"You still have things to do in Albernaith," Grandma said.

"Well, we all do," Grandpa added, alighting his horse. He picked up Ava and put her on the ground.

Grandma followed his gesture. I was right behind her.

"We're leaving the horses here?" Ava asked with a frown.

"They know the way home," Grandpa said as the horses turned around and disappeared in the woods.

"We didn't get to say goodbye to Ishmael," Ava observed.

"Why would you say goodbye?" Grandma smiled. "You'll be back soon."

"Alright, everyone." Grandpa walked to the tree and placed his hands on its bark. "Time to finish our Christmas celebration back home. We still have more cookies to eat."

Ava and Grandma followed him.

A breeze blew across the forest, the branches of the trees swaying to its rhythm. The memory of Doopar's lavender eyes filled my mind. Though the image of her dead body tried to replace my happy memory, I fought it away. "I'll always remember you," I said under a breath.

"Enzo!" Ava had her hand on the tree. "Come on."

I ran and joined them.

A thin golden line appeared, drawing the shape of the doorway. We walked into the darkness. The door behind us slammed shut as ripples appeared in the air, creating the shape of a dome. The darkness thinned, revealing the backyard I knew so well.

The four of us walked out of the tree. Streaks of orange and purple painted the sky. It was strange to return since I wasn't sure if I was ever going to see this place again. The trees surrounding their house made the image of Doopar's face more vivid in my head.

"Mr. Wombington!" Ava ran in the snow, grabbing the wet brown teddy bear from the ground.

"It was here this whole time?" I asked.

"I don't know, but I'm so happy." She frowned, holding it away from her. "It's all wet and stinky."

"Let's go inside and wash him then, okay?" Grandma said.

"We also need to change," Grandpa observed. "People might think we're confusing today with Halloween."

We walked through the massive glass door, entering the kitchen. The house was spotless. I ran to the stairs and looked up at the roof. The hole had been fixed. The Christmas tree was lit, the fireplace burning. Grandma and Ava filled up the kitchen sink with water to wash Mr. Wombington.

"I obviously used a little bit of magic to fix it up before we arrived," Grandpa said, hands on his waist.

"You have the Seeing Star?" I asked.

"No, that necklace can never enter Albernaith. I used it while still in the castle." He winked.

"How can I get used to this life again? I mean, I know I spent almost a week away in Henderbellian days, and it was almost a whole day in this world, but still, can I get used to living this ordinary life?"

"No." He smiled. "You're not the same person. You changed. It doesn't matter if it took a day or a week. You're different. No one is ever the same after taking a risk." He laid a hand on my shoulder. "But remember, magic also lives in this world."

"It does?" I scowled.

"Of course. It's in your blood. It's in you."

"Thank you, Grandpa" I said.

I made my way up the stairs while they cleaned up Mr. Wombington in the kitchen. My bag was still beside the bookshelf. The window provided a stunning view of the now orange sunset. I sat on the bed, my phone still on the nightstand. There were 3 missed calls from Mom, and an unopened direct message from Cliff on social media.

I knew calling my mom meant at least thirty minutes of explaining why we had all disappeared on Christmas day. I went straight to social media to see what Cliff wanted. It was probably another insulting remark or a degrading meme.

Feeling left every limb in my body. It was a photo. Dad held a knife to Cliff's throat. Around his neck sat a necklace with a pendant shaped like the symbol of the skull crowned with thorns. On top of the photo were the words: *THIS IS THE BEGINNING OF YOUR NIGHTMARE.*

# ACKNOWLEDGEMENTS

A grateful heart attracts countless blessings. Hopefully this page will be a major magnet for those!

My incredible, epic, and supportive family, thank you. You've been my rock during many storms and getting to have another one of these into the world is a reflection of your legendary status.

To my close friends: Though scattered around the globe, we're still connected by our everlasting bond. Know you continue to inspire me daily! Your words of inspiration and affirmation have fueled me in every way possible. But I'd like to highlight w: Mariana and Junior, thank you for naming your child You know I stole that name from you; Sasha Alsberg, ntinuous resilience to scare me inspired many scenes in el. I hope you're happy. To my dramatic coven in da, keep on brewing drama so I can always feel like I long in a soap opera. Flávia Proença, where's my dragon?

To all my incredible readers and followers, thank you for sticking around. You're the reason I get to tell stories. I love you all!

J.D.

CPSIA information can be obtained
at www.ICGtesting.com
Printed in the USA
BVHW071913131019
560925BV00003B/4/P